TRICK 13

TRICK 13

Terence Reese
and
Jeremy Flint

WEIDENFELD AND NICOLSON
LONDON

Copyright © 1979 by Terence Reese and Jeremy Flint

Published in Great Britain by
Weidenfeld and Nicolson
91 Clapham High Street, London SW4 7TA

All rights reserved. No part of this publication may be reproduced, stored in a retrieval system, or transmitted, in any form or by any means, electronic, mechanical, photocopying, recording or otherwise, without the prior permission of the copyright owner.

ISBN 0 297 77582 0

Printed in Great Britain by
Redwood Burn Ltd
Trowbridge and Esher

Contents

THE VERDICT	7
MADRID *by Elvin Starr*	10
LONDON *by Elvin Starr*	31
MIAMI *by Maurice Levine*	49
LONDON AND YORK *by Elvin Starr*	70
MONTE CARLO *by Toni Cory*	94
THE INQUIRY *by Hervey Pearson*	106
LONDON AND DEAUVILLE *by Elvin Starr*	151
THE SENTENCE	170

*For Honor and Alwyn,
with whom the apricot always blossoms.*

*Authors' Note
The book is set in the future to
avoid any reference to, or association
with, present-day players.*

The Verdict

'Your lot still out?'

Closely examined, it was not a very intelligent question. If the jury had not still been out, Tom Anstruther would have been in court and not gossiping with a colleague in one of the galleries at the Old Bailey.

'Yes, it'll be another couple of hours, I dare say,' Anstruther replied.

'Any doubt?'

'Not really. George Lewthwaite summed up pretty strongly for us. If the case goes to appeal the Defence will say that their arguments on the question of intent were not sufficiently put to the jury. What's yours?'

The last two words were not the standard invitation but a polite inquiry about the case in which his friend was engaged.

'GBH. My client's a doorman at a gaming club in Poplar. He says that when this drunken Australian came charging at him he put up his knee to protect himself. The Aussie was in hospital for three weeks.'

There was a flurry at the end of the corridor. 'Jury's coming back, Sir Thomas,' a voice called.

Anstruther looked at his watch. 'Can't be the verdict yet, they've only been out for an hour. I must fly. See you later.'

The press benches were full when Anstruther returned to the courtroom, but the atmosphere was relaxed. Nobody was expecting the verdict yet. The jury filed in, the usher called 'Be upstanding in court'; and Mr Justice Lewthwaite made his entrance, looking like an old turkey-cock. When he had made his bow and taken his seat he opened a spectacle case that was lying on his desk, adjusted his pince-nez, shut the case with a snap, and addressed the Foreman:

'I believe you have a question for me?'

The Foreman put his question impersonally, as though aware that it might sound a trifle quaint.

'Some members of the jury feel that it might be helpful if they could peruse a French dictionary, My Lord.'

A titter went round the court and the judge shook his dewlap in reproach.

'Er, yes. You could have asked the usher for that, you know. I think there is a French dictionary in my room, yes I'm sure there is. A French-English dictionary, is that what you want? The usher will bring it to you. Is that all?'

Another two hours went by. 'God knows what they're thinking about,' Anstruther remarked irritably to his junior. 'Some of these juries couldn't tell you it was raining in the middle of a thunderstorm. I wanted to get back to the country tonight.'

An hour and a half later a general stir signalled that the jury was about to return. This time every inch of space was occupied. Reporters crowded near the doors, impatient to relay the climax of a murder trial that had held the nation transfixed for three weeks.

'Be upstanding in court,' intoned the usher.

The judge went through the same performance with his spectacle case, gave his wig a tug, and nodded to the Clerk of the Court.

'Will your Foreman please stand?'

A West Indian rose solemnly to his feet.

'Do you find the prisoner –'

There was a sudden disturbance as a woman in the benches behind the defending Counsel fell forward in a dead faint. The judge held up a hand to stay the proceedings while an usher hurried forward with a glass of water. The man beside her patted her cheeks and chafed her wrists. When she appeared to recover, the Clerk repeated his question:

'Do you find the prisoner guilty or not guilty?'
'Guilty.'
'Is that the verdict of you all?'
'It is.'

Mr Justice Lewthwaite turned to the accused. 'The jury, by a unanimous verdict, has found you guilty of the offence with which you are charged. On the evidence that has been given before this court, no other verdict was possible.

'The question I have to decide now is to what extent the killing was deliberate. To clarify this point I propose to trace the events that led up to it.

'On 7 August of last year...'

Madrid

by Elvin Starr

I am sorry I have not learned to play at cards. It is very useful in life; it generates kindness and consolidates society.
DR SAMUEL JOHNSON

Balls!

I can think of half a dozen couples in the tournament world who would willingly strangle one another. Sometimes the antipathy is natural, sometimes it can be traced back to a particular incident.

There was a moment of this kind on the last day of the European Championship in Madrid. At the time it seemed to be just a 'bad board', as we bridge players say. Looking back, one can see that it was like a pebble thrown into a pond, causing ever-widening circles.

I was playing for the British team against France in the final round. At this point we were good favourites to win the championship. If we could win the present match by 15–5 or better we couldn't be overtaken by Italy or any other team. The scorer placed board 27 on the table. As it was a 32-board match there were just six hands to go. If our idiots at the other table haven't muddled it, I thought, we must be well ahead. All we needed was to avoid a calamity.

We were playing in the 'closed room', which means no spectators, only players and officials. There were 22 tables in the open series, 14 in the women's event. It was the hottest day there'd been and the air-conditioning wasn't working. Typical

Spanish! Who chose the middle of August, anyway? Matter of finance, presumably. The only windows were in the ceiling and there wasn't a breath of air. Everyone was sweating like a pig, except for my partner, Hervey Pearson. He was wearing a snazzy outfit of black trousers and green shirt, probably from the boutique at the hotel. At the next table to ours a beefy Frenchwoman was waving a toy fan in front of her ugly mug. The normal standards of pulchritude seemed to be reversed at this tournament. I mean, if it came to a parade in bathing costumes, which heaven forbid, our lot . . .

'It's your deal, Mr Starr,' the scorer reminded me gently.

'Sorry, I was dreaming.'

Before I could make my call we were interrupted by an announcement over the public address, in Spanish and English, about arrangements for the banquet in the evening.

I had drifted into this life with my eyes open. At Cambridge I studied Law, following a family tradition, but as a career it seemed too slow and I gave up. There wasn't much doing for someone with my qualifications, or lack of them. I worked on a building site at one time, learning a bit about life in the raw. As a result, my style tends to vary between donnish Dr Jekyll and earthy Mr Hyde.

I had played a lot of bridge at university and soon found there were easier ways to make a living than by hoisting bricks. Apart from bridge, I am pretty hot at backgammon and poker, and I play a nifty game of tennis. To complete the picture, I am twenty-seven, on the short side, but strong. I keep fit and go to classes in self-defence, meaning vicious attack.

When they stopped gabbling over the public address I looked at my cards for the first time and saw that I had an enormous hand, with a void in spades and seven top hearts. Very fine at rubber bridge, but dynamite at this stage of the match, when the game was to kick into touch or pass back to the goalkeeper.

The big bid in our system was one diamond, so I pressed the appropriate buttons. At the touch of a finger the call that has been made glimmers on a centre panel. This electronic system has obvious advantages – no emphasis or inflexion, no language problem, no noise. It's also supposed to cut out all charges of illegal communication. What a hope! Tables with these gadgets cost upwards of 500 (new) pounds. Well, there's money in bridge nowadays, thanks to sponsorship.

After my one diamond opening the opponents tried to shut us out by bidding high in hearts. I followed a very strong sequence but I couldn't get Hervey to budge. We finished in five spades, and when the dummy went down I saw we had missed an easy slam. Hervey could be bloody obstinate at times. No use saying anything, though.

Hervey is in his middle forties, well set up, with the poise of a man who might have been a dancer in his younger days. He is a stamp-dealer; a curious way to earn a living, but Hervey seems to do very well at it, without much effort. When we are abroad he sometimes disappears for 'a chat with a colleague in the business'. This phrase has become something of a joke.

Nothing much happened in the last five boards. The Frogs offered us strangled congratulations, then moved off, hurling reproaches at one another from a fixed distance like duellists. This set off a chorus of shushing from the tournament directors. Personally I could play bridge in the middle of Piccadilly Circus on bonfire night, but shushing completely destroys my concentration.

Hervey, who always makes a point of these little courtesies, thanked the scorer, and we set off for the conference hall to watch the tail-end of our match on bridgerama. This is an electrically operated board which enables an audience to watch everything that happens in one of the main matches. Play in the closed room is always ahead of the bridgerama room, so one gets away in time to watch the last few boards of one's own match being played at the 'other table' (where two players of the opposing team bid and play the same hands that you and your partner have just held).

The sponsors had engaged a professional commentator to assist the local talent. As soon as Hervey and I appeared he boomed into the microphone, 'Folks, I spy the Brits who have been playing in the closed room – *el torero* Hervey Pearson and *el juvenil* Elvin Starr!' I responded to the applause with a feeble wave, but Hervey carried it off perfectly with a graceful whirl and an '*olé*'.

Here the air-conditioning was working full blast, and after the hot-house of the closed room I could have done with an overcoat. The scoreboard showed that the players on bridgerama had reached board 26 and we were leading by 42 match points – more than enough for the 15–5 win we needed. (Match points are converted into victory points.) The commentator explained the exact position and concluded, 'At this moment of time it looks as though the Brits are going to be the new champs.'

As my eyes grew accustomed to the light I saw Miles Lang and Helga Rowlands sitting rump to rump a few rows in front. Helga gets that way when she's had a bit to drink, which is most of the time. Miles was a member of our team, not playing at the moment, and Helga's husband, Frank, was captain of the women's team. I found a seat behind them.

'Well done,' said Miles. 'The boys have played well, too.' The boys were Maurice Levine and Peter Rosswick, both doing postgraduate courses at Manchester University. They were the second half of our team. A team consists of three pairs and a captain. Ours was set out in the official programme as follows:

> Harvey Pearson and Elvin Starr (myself)
> Miles Lang and Leonard Fieldsman
> Maurice Levine and Peter Rosswick
> Edward Clinton (non-playing captain)

Hervey's name was misspelt, as usual, because it is pronounced that way.

Helga raised a glass and said 'Hi'.

'How did it go at the finish?' Miles asked.

'We missed an easy slam on the board coming up now', I told him. 'Not much after that.'

The opposition sailed easily into the slam that Hervey and I had missed on board 27, reducing our lead to 31. It was announced from the commentary box that Italy had whitewashed Bulgaria 20–0. We could still afford one small swing against us, but not more. The afternoon matches were mostly over by now and players from other teams were streaming into the auditorium, watching our match on bridgerama and on the closed-circuit television screens that were dotted around.

Board 28 was flat, then 29 went up. 'What did you do on this?' Miles asked, before the result from the closed room had been announced.

'They played in three no trumps. We found the best lead and held them to nine tricks. We can hardly lose on the board.'

Famous last words! Man United, as we called the Manchester boys, chose this moment for a monumental misunderstanding. Briefly, they got their wires crossed over a convention known as five-ace Blackwood and bid a slam missing two aces. As soon as it was clear they were over the top, there was a bellow from the French and Italian supporters.

This was a further 11 points to France. Our lead was down to 20. We had a chance to gain on the next deal when Levine was in a part-score contract, but it seemed to me that he misplayed it. We dropped points on the last board of the match as well, when the defence went astray. In terms of victory points we had won the match 13–7, not enough. '*Viva Italia,*' the moron at the microphone shouted over the din.

We pushed our way past rampaging Eyeties and false sympathizers and took the lift to the Players' Room on the third floor. Levine and Rosswick were already there, looking grim. We all knew the result but as usual we went through the scoresheet, marking the swings.

Nothing was said about the two fateful slams, but when we came to board 30, the part-score deal, Maurice Levine remarked:

'Sorry about that. I ought to have made it.'

'Heavens, don't blame yourself,' said Rosswick. 'You were shaken by the previous hand, very naturally.'

Unlike most bridge players, Rosswick is always willing to take the blame.

'Bad luck,' said Clinton, our non-playing captain, when we had finished comparing. 'Just the two slam hands. At least, we'll get another crack at the Italians in the Bermuda Bowl. I must find the Italian captain and congratulate him. We've got two tables at the banquet. See you there.'

Hervey's girlfriend, Toni Cory, came over from the table where the women had been checking the scores in their match.

'How did you go?' Hervey asked.

'Horrible. We lost 19–1 to Greece.' The girls had been lying third at the beginning of the day. Now they would be fifth or sixth.

It was true, as Clinton had said, that by finishing second in the open series we had qualified for the world championship, due to be played in Monte Carlo the following spring. This was because Italy, as current holders of the Bermuda Bowl, had the right to defend. As runners-up in the European Championship, we would represent the European zone.

At the moment, however, we were thinking more about the match we had just thrown away. Apart from the kudos, it was a serious financial blow for me. The main income of a tournament player comes from what are known as 'pro dates'. Partly for the experience, partly in the hope of winning 'Master Points', a palooka will charter an expert to play perhaps a single session, perhaps a Congress weekend. As a European champion I could have asked for double my present fee. The year before I had played in the championship in Cairo. (I do know that Cairo's not in Europe, but the European Bridge League casts a wide net.) One of our three pairs there was a dead-weight and we finished fifth. This year we had led the field since the first round and had thrown away the championship with two follies in the last six boards.

What with one thing and another, most of us were pretty dejected by the time the banquet at last got under way. Only Miles seemed in a good mood. Bridge players suffer from mixed emotions on these occasions. Naturally Miles was disappointed we had not won, but he was crusty at being dropped for the last set and not too displeased at the way things had turned out. The banquet at any big tournament tends to be the worst meal of the week and this one was no exception. We consoled ourselves with a liberal investment in the rough but, for my unsophisticated taste, tolerable Spanish wines.

After the banquet, the speeches. Since half the company could not readily follow English at the best of times, still less when delivered in a foreign accent over a scratchy microphone, the hum of conversation grew to a level that made any attempt to be heard quite laughable. Undeterred, various important officials delivered their set pieces. This was followed by the national anthems of the winners and runners-up in the open and women's series. God Save The King, as rendered by the Spanish band, was unrecognizable but at least it was short. The Italian anthem, on the other hand, is long and contains a notorious trap. It seems at last to come to its conclusion – bom, bompity, bom, bom, bom. Everyone except the Italian team sits down, exhausted, then it strikes up again – bompity bom, bompity bom. The Italian women had been runners-up in their section and we were all caught out again.

It was past midnight before all this was over and general dancing could be resumed. At one point only Maurice Levine and myself were left at our table. He looked like a little golliwog with his frizzy hair, smoky spectacles, frilled shirt, and red cummerbund, puffing at a cigar twice as long as himself. Still, he has brains, this one. He moved his chair nearer to mine and said:

'It was pretty dumb of Hervey not to give you six on that slam hand.'

'It certainly was.'

'Sorry about our calamity. That was horrible, when we had the championship in our pocket.'

'I don't understand how you could play this five-ace Blackwood without discussing what to do with one ace and the king of trumps.'

'Of course we had discussed it. Ross forgot, that's all.'

'Forgot! That's not like him.'

'I know.' Maurice looked round and moved a little closer. 'He wasn't well. Couldn't you see that?'

'He looked pretty sick when we were comparing scores. I dare say we all did as far as that goes.' Ross is tall and blonde with a gentle expression unusual among bridge players. He doesn't look robust at the best of times.

'He didn't know what he was doing, the last half hour.'

'Don't make a bloody mystery of it, Maurice. What was wrong with him?'

'Can't you guess? Pills.'

'Pills? Is he asthmatic or something?'

'Oh, come on,' said Maurice. 'Do you lead such a sheltered life? When exam pressure is on, half the men take pep pills. Uppers they call them.'

'I see! No wonder we couldn't win the European Championship with a bloody drug addict in the team. Why did you play the last sixteen boards if you knew he wasn't in his right mind?'

'You can never tell when the reaction will set in. I didn't know anything was wrong till that slam hand near the finish.'

People were coming back to their tables now. There were signs that some entertainment was about to take place. Spanish dancing. Without exchanging a word, Maurice and I made our escape to an adjoining lounge, from which the fandango could be faintly heard.

'Our partnership is over anyway,' said Maurice, resuming the discussion. 'Ross has been offered a lecturing job in America. He was in two minds about it, but now he has decided to go.'

This was bad news. We wouldn't find a better pair for the world championship.

'What about the Bermuda Bowl?' I asked. 'Will Ross be able to get back for that?'

'He hopes to play in the American trials, I believe. His father was British but he was born in America and went to college there. He has dual nationality.' Maurice paused. 'In a way it's all rather convenient. Does the name Habib mean anything to you?' he asked suddenly.

'Habib who?'

'Shoukry Habib. He has heard of you. He saw you playing in Cairo last year.'

'So?'

'A couple of months ago I was at Crockford's with a Manchester girl, Jilly Lucas. I have a system for roulette and I'm interested in Blackjack. At the big table an Arab was staking £500 on all seven boxes when he had the chance. He heard Jilly and me talking bridge, introduced himself, and invited us to supper. It turned out that bridge was his passion and that he had invented a bidding system, called the Habibi Heart.'

'Any good?'

'Difficult to tell how it would work out at the table, but it contains some novel ideas. I think one could make something of it. Habib knew I was in the team for Madrid and wanted Ross and me to play his system next year. I told him Ross might not be available. He said you were the only possible alternative.'

'What was the proposition?'

'He didn't discuss it at the time, but he asked me to 'phone him later at the Dorchester. We had a long talk. He suggested a retainer of £10,000 a year. He would arrange our tournament schedule, covering all expenses, and pay bonuses for any big event we won.'

This could be a solution to my financial problems, which were numerous and acute. There were a couple of post-dated cheques floating round the clubs in London which I would have to meet shortly; a casino was on the way to obtaining a judgment summons against me; and I had a long list in my diary of friends and acquaintances to whom I owed money. An income of £10,000 a year for an enterprise that would take up a lot of my time was no fortune, but the knowledge of it would help to hold my creditors at bay.

The Arab's proposition was fine up to a point, but could I ditch Hervey without doing myself a lot of harm one way or another? He would be mortally offended, apart from the fact that I owed him money. Also, I had every intention of seducing his girlfriend, Toni Cory, and a bust-up with Hervey wouldn't be the best way to set about it. I didn't need to explain any of this to Maurice. He would know what was worrying me on the bridge side, anyway. 'I'll have to think it over,' was all I said now. 'We can talk to this Habib character when we get back to London.'

The stamping and castaneting seemed to have finished, and

we returned to our table. People were drifting off and most of those who were left were looking the worse for wear. Miles's partner, Leonard Fieldsman, was shaking his head and lamenting:

'How the hell did we come to fall on our asses right at the end?'

'Like the Irishman who planned to stick up a bank,' murmured Ross, who had recovered his spirits better than most of us. Ross is famous for his Irish stories and everyone pressed him to tell this one. It was the sort of story that would look silly in print, but Ross told it brilliantly. 'Rossie, you're a dream,' said Helga, with drunken solemnity.

At a neighbouring table Julia Lang, a cousin of Miles, was staring fixedly at her partner in the women's team, Rhoda Penfold. 'I think Julia's going to ask Rhoda to dance,' remarked Frank Rowlands, who was trying to get Helga on her feet and off to bed. When Helga departed, Miles, who had been sitting with some of the Spanish players, rejoined our table.

'The Spanish boys have given me three tickets for the *corrida* tomorrow,' he said to Hervey. 'How would you and Toni like to come along?' We were not due to fly home till the day after next.

'Sorry, I can't manage it myself, I've got something else on tomorrow,' Hervey replied.

'One of your little business chats?' inquired Miles with a smile.

'Not this time. I've been roped in to help with the organization of the Youth Championship next summer. I'm meeting the Rumanian Youth Organizer tomorrow, to discuss various arrangements. Toni might like to go to the bullfight. What about you, Elvin, why don't you go instead of me?'

It was a chance to be with Toni without Hervey around. 'Could we discuss it in the morning?' I asked, not wanting to appear too keen. 'God knows how I'll be feeling.'

'You'll enjoy it,' said Miles. 'Toni's gone to bed, hasn't she? I'll ring her room in the morning. Shall we meet by the pool, about 11.30?'

When I staggered down next morning Miles was in the water

and Hervey was playing backgammon with Clinton under one of the orange-striped umbrellas.

'Toni's not down yet,' said Hervey. 'Miles is going to take you both to lunch at the Ritz. Pull up a chair and pick up a few hints.'

I perched uncomfortably on a metal chair. After his next throw Hervey reached a position where the pro game is to hit on the 1-point, playing for a double game. Hervey played the roll safely, bringing out his last back man. Clinton then rolled 1-6, which would have been a devastating reply if Hervey had made the other play. Hervey smiled and said to me:

'You would have hit on the 1-point, wouldn't you?'

So Hervey had seen the other play and rejected it. I found that interesting. It doesn't do to underestimate Hervey.

The sun was burning the back of my neck, so I dived stylishly into the pool and began some frolicsome exchanges with Rhoda Penfold. Rhoda is a fair, straight-up-and-down little thing, quite attractive if you like the Peter Pan type. It was easy to understand that she would appeal to a woman like Julia Lang. Rumour had it that she was playing ingenue parts in local rep when Julia picked her up.

'I'm off to change now,' called Miles from the edge of the pool. 'We're meeting in the hall at 1.15.'

I selected light grey trousers and a blue shirt for the occasion. Miles was already in the lobby when I came down.

'According to Hemingway, anybody who is anybody lunches at the Ritz before an important *corrida*,' he observed.

It was characteristic of Miles to mock convention and at the same time follow it. He is about forty and carries with him the aura of country house parties in the Noel Coward era – 'anyone for tennis?' sort of thing. At the moment he was studying the racing pages of an English newspaper.

'Isn't racing a bit of a mug's game?' I asked him. 'How can you beat the betting tax on top of the bookmakers' percentage?'

'It's a mug's game for mugs,' he replied complacently.

Fifteen minutes later we were on our second glass of Manzanilla and still waiting for Toni to appear. 'The señorita will be down in a very little moment,' reported one of the boys from the porter's desk. After a further ten minutes she emerged from the lift, small and slender, looking a picture in a simple apricot dress, with a dark brown necklace that matched her hair and wide eyes. I thought there might be signs of a hangover, but she was her usual bright self. 'Good morning! Sorry if I'm a little late,' she volunteered.

Miles, who had been drinking fairly steadily throughout the morning, surveyed her quizzically. 'It's only that I booked a table for ten minutes ago,' he said. 'It's a mystery to me why you women take so long to get dressed.'

Toni evidently had experience in repelling this particular attack. 'Do you suppose Helen would have launched a thousand ships in a pair of jeans?' she asked.

'As witty as she is beautiful,' laughed Miles. 'It's not far to the Ritz. Shall we walk?'

Toni looked doubtfully at her sandals, but Miles was not in a mood to indulge her. As we walked along the tree-lined avenues, I tried to analyze my feelings for Toni. There were contradictions in her nature, and in her situation, that I found fascinating. In most ways she had the lightest touch, yet at the bridge table she was a tough little cookie; it was like seeing a pretty girl at the wheel of a powerful car. There was something virginal about her, yet she was living with an older man. How strongly was she attached to Hervey? Usually I am confident when I go after a girl, but Toni was a challenge.

The light breeze, and the fountains in the Puerta Del Sol, afforded some protection from the blazing sun, but it was a relief to enter the cool of the hotel. I saw why Miles had described the Ritz as one of the last bastions of civilization. In the handsome restaurant an ancient waiter handed each of us a large menu, all in Spanish. Miles did his worldly bit, ordering for everyone. We had gazpacho, paella, and oranges in liqueur.

'We have time for a *fine*,' said Miles when we reached the coffee stage. We both declined. 'Are you sure?' he went on. 'You ought to try the Spanish brandy, Elvin. It's supposed to have an aphrodisiac effect.'

'Not necessary in his case, from what I hear,' Toni put in waspishly.

'Floats like a butterfly, stings like a bee,' quoted Miles, who was pretty mellow by this time.

The drive from the hotel to the bullring was a nightmare. Each time the traffic came to a halt, the drivers engaged in a furious contest of horn-blowing. Miles cursed our taxi, which ought to have been air-conditioned but wasn't, the police, the roads, even the newly-elected government.

'Our seats are in the *Gradas*,' he informed us when we eventually arrived at the stadium. 'You get the best view from a little way up. Like sitting in the dress circle at Covent Garden,' he added, well knowing that the comparison would be lost on me.

Every seat was taken and the crowd was in boisterous mood. The vendors of nuts, beer, cushions, programmes, ice-cream and – in midsummer – hamburgers added to the general din, not to mention the smell. We gathered from the programme that we were to see six bulls and that their two-legged opponents would be Gitanillo de Corda, Manolo Vasquez and Rafael Novarro.

The band struck up a stirring *paso doble*, signalling the start of the parade. It was led by two overdressed ponces in some kind of ancient court dress. Then, to tumultuous applause, came the three matadors in gold silk suits, followed by the foot-soldiers, or peons, dressed predominantly in silver. Next were the picadors on their padded horses, and finally the mule teams and assorted underlings. I had a sudden thought that the man with a shovel who follows the greyhounds at White City would have added a homely touch to the proceedings. When the parade reached the President's box the two poufs doffed their plumed hats and the train marched slowly off, leaving just Gitanillo and his peons in the ring. The President waved a handkerchief, the gate opened, and the first bull made a thunderous entrance. I don't know much about bulls, but this one certainly seemed to belong to a different species from the animal that roamed the fields near my home village in Norfolk.

The matador performed a number of elegant passes, the

peons and picadors provoked the animal in various ways, then Gitanillo strode across to the President's box and did his *moriturus te saluto* act. The crowd was ready for the kill by this time. Gitanillo stood at an angle, his sword-arm extended like a tennis player frozen in a high backhand volley. As the bull followed the *muleta* – the proverbial red rag – Gitanillo killed it with his first thrust.

To me it seemed neatly done, but there were whistles and yells of 'Assassin!' According to Miles, the matador had shifted his position in some unethical manner. 'I think they're beastly to him,' cried Toni, applauding wildly as Gitanillo left the ring with the injured air of a footballer who had been shown the red card for some imaginary offence.

The next performer, Vasquez, was off to a great start. One of his peons laid a cape on the sand in front of the bull and hared for the barricade. He didn't quite make it and had his pantaloons ripped off by the angry beast. Then one of the picadors was thrown from his horse and Vasquez made a swift and heroic intervention to save the man from being gored.

Suddenly the whole atmosphere changed. The bull stood rooted to one spot, ignoring all challenges. 'Ah,' said Miles, 'this is interesting. The bull has established what they call a *querencia*. It has developed a liking for the spot where the picador was thrown and it won't budge from there. I haven't seen this before.'

Vasquez was now in something of a dilemma. If he was not to look a fool, he had to lure the bull from its chosen spot. He inched closer and closer to provoke a charge, but the brute perversely stood its ground, watching but not moving. 'No! No!' screamed the crowd at each cautious step, meaning, like a woman, 'Yes! Yes!' Toni gripped my arm, drawing her breath in quick gasps. At last the bull charged, hooking violently to the left and ripping a wide gash in the green and gold suit. Minions rushed into the ring and were angrily waved aside by Vasquez, who had escaped serious injury.

Master of the situation again, Vasquez performed a series of artistic movements, finishing with one that was supposed to 'fix' the bull. Over-confident, he turned his back on the animal to acknowledge the frantic applause. The bull now unsportingly charged from the blind side and tossed him high in the air. From a recumbent position the wounded hero again waved back the peons, but blood was pouring from his thigh and he was carried off on a stretcher. Immediately the next matador, Novarro, entered the ring with a purposeful air and despatched the beast with a single stroke.

Well, I thought, they won't top that: the peon scrambling bare-assed over the barricade, the dramatic rescue of the picador, the *querencia*, the tossing of Vasquez, the kill by Novarro. I saw that Toni was pale and shaken. 'Have you had enough?' I asked her. 'Do you want to leave?'

'Oh, yes,' she said. 'But what about the people who gave us the tickets?'

'Don't worry about that,' said Miles. 'I'm meeting the Spanish boys after the show. I'll tell them you left just before the end as you wanted to get back to the hotel to do your packing.'

It was too early for a meal. 'Let's go to the Prado for a couple of hours,' Toni suggested, as we settled into a taxi.

'The who?'

'The Prado. It has a super collection of Velasquez and Goyas.'

I wasn't going to be dragged round any bloody museum. I told her I had promised the proprietor to look in at Manuel's, a coffee bar on the outskirts of the town where various games were played. 'Everything's going my way,' I sang to myself as we hurtled along the now empty roads. Take her out to supper, get her pissed, I couldn't miss.

From Manuel's we went to a dive called La Guitarria. The restaurant looked just right for my purpose: check tablecloths, candlelight, dubious representations of Andalucian art on the walls, a swinging band with a negro singer. After wrestling with some langoustine we took to the dance floor.

Dancing is not one of my better accomplishments. My system during the rock numbers is to move into a sort of indeterminate shuffle and watch my partner's antics with a wolfish grin. As I followed Toni back to our table at the end of the number I let my fingertips rest on her soft buttocks, still warm from her exertions. She moved away and when we took our seats a slight frown settled on her delicate brow. A little hoarsely, I asked her:

'Who was it who said that dancing was a vertical expression of a horizontal thought?'

'Father Time,' she snapped.

All right, snubbed with a snub! There are worse fates.

The conversation, in so far as it was possible to converse in this racket, moved to Toni's entry into the bridge world. She had played since childhood. Her father, an antique dealer with a business in York, had been a county player and was now chairman of the Yorkshire Association. She had met Hervey at a Northern Congress and he had told her that the way to put an edge on her game was to play in London. Not a bad variation on 'Come up and see my etchings,' I thought. After a few weeks she had moved into Hervey's apartment.

'I still work for the firm,' she added. 'I go to auctions and pick up good pieces.' She was telling me that Hervey didn't keep her.

Toni's partner in the women's team was an old trout from Yorkshire, called Laura Durston. I asked her how they had got on and whether she felt the team ought to have done better.

'Of course,' she answered. 'We could easily have been second, even on the last day. I think Laura and I played as well as anyone expected us to. It was Julia.'

'Julia? I thought that, present company excepted, she was the best player in the team.' Julia, who is in her thirties, smart and assured, plays regularly in the high game at our club in London.

'Don't try to flannel me, Starr. Julia is a class above the rest of us, we all know that. But didn't you know the drama that was going on?'

'Nobody tells me anything.'

'That's because you're such an old gossip and mischief-maker. Anyway, you only had to use your eyes. Rhoda's been having an affair with that Spaniard, Lopez. Haven't you seen them together?'

'I suppose I have, now you mention it, but it didn't register particularly. Is Jellier juic . . .?' I tried again: 'Is Juici . . . is Julia jealous?'

'Fiendishly. She has given Rhoda such hell the last two days the poor girl hasn't been able to play a single right card.'

'Funnily enough, I had a tickle with Rhoda myself in the pool this morning.'

'You're lucky Julia didn't see you. One day last week that Belgian girl, Jeannine, was laughing and splashing with Rhoda. Julia dropped her cigarette holder, flung off her robe, and swam towards them to break it up. Like a shark, no less.' Toni giggled. 'It's the only time I've known her get wet. Now let's change the subject.'

When people say 'let's change the subject' it usually means they are on the point of telling you something interesting. Toni was fairly well tanked up by now and after extracting numerous pledges of secrecy she went on:

'The sad thing is that Rhoda's not gay at all. She's as straight as a ruler. But Julia, well, dominates her.'

'In what way?'

'Oh, Elvin, I'll kill you if you tell anybody. I had the room next to theirs at Monte Carlo in March. One of those rickety old-fashioned hotels. I couldn't help hearing.'

Restraining my impatience at this cautious approach, I asked in a level tone: 'Hearing what?'

'Whacks.'

'Wax?'

'Yes, whacks. I said something to Rhoda about funny noises and she talked quite freely. After every session of bridge Julia goes through the scorecard with her and marks off her mistakes. If they get to the wrong contract it's always Rhoda's fault. Julia uses some system of crosses and each one means a spanking, or worse. She makes Rhoda bend over the bed and lays into her with a leather switch or a hairbrush. And after Rhoda had been seen here with this Spaniard, Julia began to make her crosses at the table. Rhoda lost her nerve altogether, and no wonder.'

This was the best gossip I had heard for months. Rhoda has a nice bunched-up little ass, and the thought of Julia crimsoning her bare behind was interesting. I wondered if I could get into that game myself one day. 'Why does Rhoda put up with it?' I asked.

'She says it sort of developed gradually. And she's in a difficult position. Julia pays for everything on these trips.'

I couldn't extract any more details.

'Tell me about yourself,' Toni said. 'You're ambitious, aren't you?'

'In the sense that I mean to get to the top in bridge, yes.'

'What does your family think of it all?'

'Not much. I left Cambridge without taking a degree, which didn't please them, though I must say they spared me the "after all the sacrifices we've made" bit. My older brother is at the Bar, which from their point of view is both more respectable and more profitable.'

We had reached the coffee stage now. The trumpet player had put his instrument aside and was investigating the fleas in his hair. There were signs that the cabaret was about to begin. Notices outside the restaurant had proclaimed a singer named Veronica Lee. I had visions of a toothsome American doll, but Miss Lee turned out to be a middle-aged Spanish female whose speciality was a kind of high Moorish wailing. Shutting my mind away from this, I considered my next move.

In romantic fiction the logistics of seduction are seldom considered. Once maidenly resistance has been overcome, no one stops to consider precisely where the lucky couple are to enjoy the fruits of their passion. In my experience this is often tricky. My original idea of taking Toni back to the hotel and letting nature take its course wouldn't work. At best, she would be nervous of Hervey down the corridor, the telephone might ring, there might be a knock on the door. But I could take her to one of the airport hotels, where they will let you have a room for a couple of hours on the pretence that you are freshening up after your journey. Best to go straight there, I thought, without telling her anything.

I signalled for the bill, but the waiter shrugged his shoulders and gestured in the direction of the singer. We would have to sit it out. Eventually there was a loud roll from the band and Miss Lee left the floor to scattered applause. Predictably, she fluttered back as though overwhelmed by her reception and launched into the second half of her performance.

When at last we were able to escape, Toni swaying a little at the impact of the fresh air, I chartered a taxi and quietly instructed the driver, in my rudimentary Spanish, to drive to an airport hotel. Before we had gone any distance he began to air his English, in the way that foreign taxi-drivers sometimes do.

'Your Priminister good man – yes, no?' he began.

The last thing I wanted was a conversation with the driver, so instead of assenting to this dubious proposition I broke into a flow of pseudo-Hungarian – a tactic I had used on previous occasions.

'Man think we Inglesi,' I added for Toni's benefit.

'Naji pu,' she exclaimed, responding in similar gibberish.

The driver huffily closed the partition. Toni slumped sideways and showed signs of falling asleep. I knew she wouldn't like the idea of going to another hotel for a quickie and my plan was to get her so randy that when we arrived she would want to head straight for the nearest bedroom.

To begin with, I had to get her upright. I took out a cigarette, leaned over her, and placed it between her lips. I flicked my lighter and she had to sit up so that I could light the cigarette. I put my arm around her waist and kept up a flow of conversation so that she wouldn't notice where we were going.

When she had finished the cigarette she leaned her head on my shoulder and I began to kiss her hair and the nape of her neck. I moved my right hand slowly upwards, just brushing the outside of her breast. When this passed off without protest I edged my hand towards the centre, lightly squeezing the nipple between my first and second finger. Then I brought my left hand across to her other breast and my right hand moved down her body. She was leaning sideways, with her bottom at an angle to the seat and her dress rucked up. With my palm against the cheek of her trim little bottom, I extended my fingers to raise her dress still further and in a few moments I was able to touch bare skin. I thought, just an inch or two further and she'll be a pushover when we reach the hotel.

At this moment the fool of a driver, reaching the motorway after the restraints of traffic and lights, suddenly accelerated with a jerk that threw Toni backwards with her legs in the air. Sleepy or not, she realized that we were no longer threading our way through the busy streets in the centre of the city. 'What the hell's going on?' she demanded.

'I thought we might go for a drive before returning to the hotel,' I said feebly.

'Don't be so damned silly,' she said. Banging on the glass partition, she told the driver to go back to our hotel "immediamente", which sounded more Italian than Spanish. It was several minutes before the driver was able to turn off and proceed at equal speed in the opposite direction.

Toni settled into the far corner of the taxi and brought out a mirror for repairs. Cursing the driver, I resolved not to add one peseta to the fare shown on the meter.

When we got back to the hotel, Hervey and Clinton were still at their marathon game of backgammon. Had Hervey stayed up to see us come in? It was possible. Peter Rosswick was watching.

'Hullo there,' Hervey called. 'We're on our last game. How was the bullfight?'

'It was quite an experience,' I said. 'Funny in parts.'

'Frightening but exciting,' was Toni's verdict.

'Pity and terror, the components of tragedy, according to Aristotle,' remarked Clinton, more erudite than most of us.

Clinton turned the cube and Hervey surrendered. 'What have you done with Miles?' Hervey asked.

'He's gone to a nightclub with the Spanish boys,' I replied. Let Hervey assume that Miles had spent the evening with us. 'How did you get on with your Youth Organizer?'

'Oh, Frank and I spent most of the afternoon with him,' said Hervey, snapping shut the backgammon board. 'It was that little chap with the forked beard who scored for the Rumanian team. You called him Trotsky, remember? This will amuse you: when we discussed accommodation for the Eastern bloc he stipulated that in any case were there to be all boys or all girls in any of the huts; they had to be mixed. The new morality!'

We all laughed. 'One way to deal with the population problem,' Ross remarked.

'Population or copulation?' I put in.

'If they were to adopt that system for all the teams, perhaps you would change your mind and play, Elvin?' suggested Hervey with a smile.

I did not have to take this seriously. I was technically within the age limit (twenty-seven is considered young in bridge), but anyone who has played in the European Championship is not required, or even expected, to play in the junior event. I had done my stint in the wilds of Turkey two years ago, playing with a Scottish youth who was now at medical school, learning to butcher people instead of bridge hands.

'I'm off to bed,' said Hervey. 'The bus is supposed to be picking us up at nine tomorrow. Coming, Toni?'

She said goodnight to me with a murmur of thanks for the evening. I had made a fool of myself, that was certain. Not so much the business in the taxi — she could have stopped that if she had wanted to; but I was mad to think I could rush her off to a strange hotel whether she fancied the idea or not. Still, I didn't think my mistake was fatal, or that the campaign was lost. One down at half time, perhaps, but still everything to play for.

London

by Elvin Starr

The driver who was supposed to pick us up the next morning didn't appear till after 9.30. He was a good judge, because when we got to Madrid airport we had to wait another hour before boarding.

As I thought he might want to discuss the Habib project, I took a seat next to Maurice Levine. Maurice demanded the seat nearest the gangway, for a reason that soon became clear.

'What do you think of those?' he asked, golliwoggling at the Spanish stewardess as she moved down the aisle.

'I'm more of a legs and bum than a tit man,' I told him.

As the girl went by, Maurice swivelled round to survey her ass. Odd how randy these very small men sometimes are. Maurice is barely five feet high.

After inspecting the rest of the talent Maurice took out a paperback entitled *Bride of the Beast* and began to read, ignoring the screech of the engines as the pilot went through his interminable ground routine. At last the plane taxied along the runway and in a few seconds the cars on the motorway looked like a line of scurrying ants. Most of the others in our party settled down to study the hand records of our last two matches. Preferring to forget these, I gave my mind to the question of how, assuming that Maurice and I were going to come to an agreement with the Arab, I was going to break the news to Hervey.

To terminate a bridge partnership can be a traumatic experience, worse than the average divorce. In this case there was the further complication that Hervey was expecting to play with me in the World Championship, or at any rate in the trials. Hervey's wounded feelings were not the only problem. I had to be careful not to give an opening to rivals in the bridge world who would jump at the opportunity to label me a selfish and unreliable partner. I also had to consider whether or not to speak to Hervey before fixing any deal with Habib.

To some extent these problems settled themselves a few days after we got back from Madrid. A few weeks ago I had given a post-dated cheque to a wretched little man called Mosey and I wanted to ask him not to put it in just yet. I knew I'd find him at Knaves, a club in Knightsbridge. When I arrived at the club, Mosey was playing in a high-stake game that was destined to have far-reaching consequences. I don't play much rubber bridge myself because the club imposes a weekly tax on winnings, making the game a doubtful proposition for professionals.

Frank Rowlands, who captained the women's team in Madrid, and Mosey were playing against Miles Lang and Klaus Ellerman. Mosey's real name is Bruno Moisevitch. He sniffs around the money markets and is often seen in conspiratorial discourse with clients who have money to invest. Klaus Ellerman is an amiable buffoon. He represents a firm of German toy manufacturers. Although he spends half his time in England he still speaks with the accent and idiom of a stage Teuton.

Mosey is the world's most selfish and pig-headed player. A deal came along where he had a long suit of spades and Rowlands, his partner, had a long suit of hearts. Frank bid hearts three times, but Mosey stubbornly persisted with his spades, was doubled in four spades and lost 800. Frank looked annoyed but didn't say anything.

On the next deal Mosey again opened one spade. I was sitting behind Frank, who had seven hearts and a *singleton* spade. After a pass by the next player Frank raised to four spades! Klaus doubled and all passed.

When the dummy went down, with a singleton spade, Mosey exploded: 'What's this? One spade – four spades, with seven hearts and a singleton spade! What the devil are you doing?'

Frank: 'Saving time.'

The contract went two down, a further 500 to the opposition. Four hearts would have been a lay-down. Miles then made a generous offer:

'You've made your little demonstration, Frank,' he said. 'We won't take the penalty. We'll call the hand a wash-out. Do you agree, partner?'

Klaus, who detested Mosey, pretended not to understand.

'What you say?' he cried. 'What is this wash-out? I not know wash-out. I know two down doubled 500 is.' And he firmly entered the score.

'Correct,' said Frank. 'Now let's get on to the next hand.' So the score went down as 500, while Mosey muttered angrily about reporting the incident to the committee.

The rubber ended soon afterwards and the table broke up. I decided that it would not be a good moment to tackle Mosey about the cheque. Instead, I transferred my attention to a table where Hervey Pearson and Virginia Trupp were playing against Julia Lang, looking severe in one of her tailored suits, and Panos Spiliatakos. Panos has black hair sprouting from every visible part of his body. He is known as 'Orrible 'Airy, one of the cleaning woman having been overheard confiding to a colleague, "E's 'orrible 'airy.' Virginia Trupp is a tall, bird-like woman. Rain or shine, fashionable or not, she invariably wears a hat with an overhanging feather. A massive overbidder, she gave away two big penalties while I was watching.

When the session ended, Mrs Hopcraft, the old girl who acts as hostess for the £1 and £2 games, attempted to find a partner for Trupp in the £2 partnership which is held on Tuesday evenings. 'Miss Trupp wants a partner for tonight,' she announced as she bustled round emptying ashtrays and tidying up scorepads. 'What about you, Mr Ellerman, are you free? No? Elvin, just think what a thrill it would be for Virginia to play with you ... Oh, naughty ... Mrs Rowlands, would you care to play partnership with Miss Trupp?'

'You'd better put an advertisement in the *Financial Times*, Hoppy,' said Frank.

Later in the evening I came across Hervey in the bar. It seemed a good opportunity to broach the question of our future partnership. After a word about his experiences with Trupp in the afternoon, I said:

'Did you hear that Man United were breaking up? Ross is going to America shortly.'

'Yes, I know. He told me he might be able to get away for Monte Carlo, but I understand the selectors have decided to hold trials. They're not prepared to pick our team as it stands.'

'What do you suppose Maurice will do?'

'He sometimes plays with that lad from Yorkshire, doesn't he? Bruce something-or-other?'

'He's useless. Maurice only plays with him because they were at school together. Does anyone know what form the trials will take?'

'Edward thinks it will be a team trial, with our team in the box.'

Hervey meant that there would be an eliminating contest for three or four invited teams, from which our team would be exempted. The winners would have the right to challenge us to a long match. Edward, as a member of the British Bridge League Council, would surely know what was intended.

'I'd rather have Maurice on our side than against us, wouldn't you?' I said. 'Do you think there's anything to be said for forming a threesome?'

A team usually consists of three pairs, but it is also possible for three players to make up a threesome, alternating partnerships.

'I've never played with Maurice,' Hervey replied. 'It's short notice to form a new partnership.'

'We could get a fourth and play at Marbella in January, interchanging partners.'

'That's not a convenient time for me from a business point of view. There are some important auctions coming up, which I must attend. I've got another idea. Edward has asked me to play with him in the Grandmasters Pairs. We've won it twice, you know, and Edward doesn't play a lot these days. You could have a run-through with Maurice.'

This was developing rather well. If it could be made to appear that Hervey himself had suggested the new line-up, the transition might be effected without an open breach. I pretended to give Hervey's idea some consideration, then said:

'Very well. I'll sound out Maurice and see if he's free.'

'By the way,' Hervey went on, 'Toni's father is coming to town at the end of the month and we're giving a little party for him on the twenty-sixth. We won't be sending out formal invitations but we hope you'll be able to come.'

'Just let me look at my diary. I think it's all right. Yes, a Wednesday, isn't it?'

I had my back to the door and as I was speaking Arthur Mainwaring, the club bore, had come into the bar. A gaunt sixty-odd, he has the button-holing propensities of the Ancient Mariner, whose initials he shares. He must have heard the tail-end of our conversation, so Hervey, who had known him for twenty years, was trapped.

'Arthur, just the man I wanted to see. Come and join us for a drink. Toni and I are giving a little party on the twenty-sixth and we would be delighted if you could come.'

Arthur made a business of going through his list of social engagements, then said yes, it would be a great pleasure, and how was the charming little lady.

A few days later Maurice called me from Manchester. 'Habib wants us to meet him at the Dorchester next Monday,' he said. 'Can you make it? Good. Shall we meet in the lobby of the Cumberland at twenty to five? See you then.'

My pad is in Bayswater, so the Cumberland was more or less on my way. While we were walking down Park Lane I told Maurice the gist of my conversation with Hervey. He nodded but made no comment.

'About this meeting with Habib,' he said. 'You'll find him a bit, well, oblique. He may not say anything about a contract at this stage. Leave the business side to me. A few thousand years of experience, you know. This afternoon he'll give us a long spiel about his system. Pretend to be impressed.'

Maurice was looking more quaint than usual, in a check jacket that drew attention to his lack of inches. The reception clerk at the Dorchester did a double-take when we announced our business. He made a phone call, then with a distant air instructed a green-jacketed pageboy to take us to the Ptolemy suite on the 48th floor of the new Tower Block. The boy regarded Maurice with amusement, enjoying our discomfiture as the lift shot up at ninety miles an hour and came to a stop with a heart-swallowing jerk. In the corridor he asked our names, and when the door to Habib's suite was opened he announced us with some ceremony.

We entered a large room decorated in black and white, the functional style relieved by oriental rugs. Through the long window at the back we could see the trees in Hyde Park.

Habib's appearance was a surprise. I had expected something from the Arabian Nights, or perhaps a villainous sheik from the silent films. Instead, he was tall and immaculately dressed in a conservative blue suit. Apart from his brown complexion, he was the image of a city businessman. He began with a courteous little speech:

'Mr Levine, Mr Starr, how kind of you to call. I had the pleasure of meeting Maurice at Crockford's one evening, with his delightful companion, Miss Lucas, and though you wouldn't have noticed me I watched you play in Cairo last year. May I call you Elvin? My name is Shoukry. And this is my friend, Rosanna.'

Rosanna (I learned later how she came to have an Italian name) had opened the door when we came in. She was everyone's idea of the sultan's favourite. When she moved, her flowing dress, pulled in at the waist, drew the eye to her voluptuous curves. I realized that I had lost Maurice's attention.

'Unfortunately,' Habib went on, as Rosanna produced drinks and sweetmeats, 'I have a business appointment later in the afternoon, so I will come quickly to the point. As Maurice will have told you, I am hoping that you will do me the honour of playing my system, the Habibi Heart. First, let me say that playing this system I have had many successes in important tournaments, not only in Egypt but also in Tel-Aviv and Abu Dhabi. I mention this so that you will know you are not buying what I believe is called a pig in a poke. Do you know what a poke is, by the way? No? It means a bag or pouch in which the pig is concealed.' He chuckled, well pleased at being able to give us this item of information.

For the next twenty minutes he described his system. It certainly had some novel features. In first or second position a *pass* signified the values for an opening bid. Thus any opening bid except one heart, which was strong, depicted a mediocre hand with certain distributional features. One could see that such a system would create problems for the opposition.

While Habib was describing his methods Rosanna, no fool, had withdrawn to her inner chamber. She reappeared now, pushing a trolley laden with exotic dishes. There was a pot of Beluga caviare and a sort of compressed cod's roe. Habib pressed me to sample *bec figues*, little birds so called because they eat figs. Maurice, who was consuming them with relish, nodded agreement. I chose the smallest on view. In a moment my mouth was full of a horrible mish-mash of bones. On the pretence of admiring the view I went to the balcony and deposited the remains in my handkerchief.

As I came back into the room the telephone rang. 'It's reception,' said Rosanna. 'There are some people waiting to come up.'

Habib let fly a couple of sentences in Arabic. Rosanna made a face and purred into the telephone. 'Please tell the people that Mr Habib is in conference. Would they be so kindly as to wait downstairs for a few minutes?'

'Is that really what Shoukry said?' I asked.

Rosanna giggled and replied: 'No. He said "Let the sons of whores moulder in a manure heap".'

I was beginning to warm to this girl.

'But seriously,' said Habib, 'these oil buyers are most

inconsiderate people. Alas, time has flown all too quickly during this very pleasant conversation. Permit me to present each of you with a summary of the Habibi Heart. Perhaps you will be kind enough to study it before our next meeting?'

Summary! It was at least three hundred pages, weightily bound in vellum.

We thanked Shoukry and Rosanna for their kind hospitality and departed. As we left the hotel I said to Maurice:

'It's all very well, but what about the cash? I don't want to wade through all this and find there's nothing for us at the end of it.'

'Just leave that to your uncle Moishe,' said Maurice. 'All Habib wants to know before he signs the deal is that we have studied his system and intend to play it. So read it, and I'll be in touch in a few days. I have to go back to Manchester now.'

'Happy dreams of the Sultana,' I called after him as he boarded a taxi for Kings Cross.

I looked at the 'summary' once or twice during the next few days, but it was badly presented and difficult to understand.

I wondered whether it would be politic to say anything to Hervey at this stage. In the end I remarked casually that Maurice wanted to try out a new system when he played with me.

A couple of days later I was woken by the phone ringing. 'Maurice here,' said the voice. 'What do you think of it?'

'Think of what?' I was annoyed at being woken so early, especially after a late and unsuccessful night at the club.

'Of the system, of course. Wake up, this call is costing me money.'

'Hold on, I'll get the bloody thing.' I shuffled across the room and returned with arms laden.

'This forcing pass is going to be tricky against good opponents, especially when vulnerable,' I said. 'They can lie in wait and trap you, can't they? And some of the two-way bids are very much exposed to intervention.'

'What did you think of his system of negative doubles after the one spade opening? Pages 224-226.'

'We'll need to do some work on that,' I said cautiously.

'That's the point. For him, it's holy writ. To get the deal fixed up, we've got to undertake to play the system as it stands.'

'Then we'll undertake. By the way, do you think there's any chance of a £1,000 advance? A sort of signing-on fee, compensation for cancelled pro dates, that sort of thing.'

'Possible. I'll do my best. See you at Hervey's party next week. Bye for now.'

A thousand pounds would give me space for manoeuvre, I could put two of my four bank accounts into the black, so that they'd stand for a fair-sized cheque. Then I could catch up with the rent, which was overdue, and my more pressing debts. Mosey was still on my back and it might be a good tactical move to pay Hervey part of what I owed him.

Hervey's flat is in Pont Street, so on the following Monday Klaus Ellerman and I strolled along from the club. The party was already swinging when we arrived. It was mostly bridge people, but there were a few outsiders. Maurice was there with his bird from Manchester, who topped him by several inches. After a word with the hosts and a duty spell with an ancient aunt I sought him out. With the usual cocktail-party chatter surrounding us, it was possible to talk without being overheard.

'Things have been humming,' Maurice said. 'I rang Habib and told him we were ready to go ahead. His solicitors are preparing a contract on the basis we discussed earlier: £10,000 a year retainer, all expenses paid, bonus of at least £500 for any event we win.'

'Any place money?'

'No. Funny you should use that phrase. He remarked that anyone could remember the names of Derby winners, very few the names of the runners-up. In his view, only winning counts.'

'What about the signing-on fee?'

'I had a little trouble about that. He accepted it in your case, but he knew I didn't do much in the way of pro dates. I explained that I would have to move to London and abandon my post-graduate course, that sort of thing. In the end he said he would pay this fee as soon as he was satisfied that we both had a thorough knowledge of the system. He meant you.'

'It's so badly set out.'

'I know. I'll rewrite it for you if you like.'

'Thank you, that'll help. When do we start?'

'That's the other thing. He wants us to play in the Winter Nationals at Miami, three weeks from now. Ross will be in America by then. He has been in touch with his old partner, Rhett Brindley, and they'll make up a team with us. They won the inter-collegiate thing a couple of years ago.'

'Three weeks? It doesn't leave much time for visas and vaccination and fingerprints and all that sort of nonsense.'

'It leaves plenty of time. The only thing that's worrying me is whether you will ever learn the system properly.'

Before I could express my indignation at this wounding lack of trust there was a loud burst of laughter from a group with Miles Lang at the centre. 'What was all that about?' I asked Helga Rowlands, who was passing by.

'It was Miles's epitaph on Virginia,' she explained. 'I've heard it before:

> For here she lies, Virginia Trupp,
> A spinster of this town,
> Who spent her mornings getting up,
> Her evenings going down.'

'Oh, I like that! You're looking very dishy tonight, Helga,' I added. She was, too, in a red dress that set off her black hair and slim figure. I may have given the impression earlier that Helga is a bit of a man-eater. She's good fun usually, it's only when she's had too much to drink that she becomes tiresome. On the last day at Madrid she latched on to Miles with a latch, but I think that was mainly because she wasn't getting any attention from Frank.

I was talking to Klaus a few minutes later when I felt a tug at my sleeve. It was Toni, already a bit high.

'Elvin, I want your opinion about a hand,' she said. Someone had picked up one of the daily bulletins from Madrid — bridge players are like that — and had remarked on a bid made by Toni in the match against Spain. Hervey had taken sides against her and Toni was furious. She had folded the page so that I could see only the South hand:

♠ A Q 10 7 5 2
♡ 8 5 3
♢ 7 6 4
♣ 2

'It's love all, partner opens one club and the next hand overcalls with four hearts. What do you bid?'

It is the sort of question that is difficult to answer away from the table. A case could be made for double, pass, or four spades. Playing for time, I said:

'It's not so easy. What do you think, Klaus?'

'I am most pleased that you are asking me,' he replied. 'You have been seeing me play at the rubber bridge only. At the duplicate I am a most cunning calculator. I am three times champion of my home club in Gelsenkirchen. I will tell you my answer to this problem. My partner must be without hearts. I am not to be shut down: it is four spades I am bidding.'

'H'm,' I said. 'Partner is likely to be short in hearts, I agree. Still, four spades is a bit of a flier.' (I didn't think this was Toni's style.) 'The alternatives are pass or double.'

'You don't think it's wrong to pass?' said Toni quickly.

'Certainly not,' I said, seeing which way the wind was blowing. 'If partner is strong he can reopen with a double and then you have two choices, both good.'

'Hervey, you pompous prig,' Toni called across the room. 'Elvin agrees with my pass.'

Hervey was neither pompous nor a prig, and it wasn't in character for Toni to start a slanging match at her own party. The ancient aunt looked shocked.

'Show him the full hand,' Hervey called back.

'Oh, it's not interesting,' said Toni. I had caught a glimpse of the result by now. Four hearts had gone three down undoubled, while at the other table the Spanish had landed four spades on the North-South cards.

'Hervey's been insufferable all day,' Toni informed me. 'It started at breakfast when he read that a cover sent from New Zealand to London in 1858, consisting of a green shilling stamp cut in half to pay sixpence postage, had been sold at auction for over £10,000. He has some similar oddities and proposes to put them on the market at two-yearly intervals. A cover means a stamp together with the envelope and postmark, in case you didn't know.' She yawned. 'Personally I'm bored with this party. What about you?'

At this very promising moment Arthur Mainwaring descended on us. 'Aha, the beauteous Antoinette,' he began, wafting gin in all directions. 'What's this hand you're all talking about? Let's see what your Uncle Arthur would have done.'

As though anyone could care less what Uncle Arthur would have done on this or any other hand. Toni moved off on the pretext of welcoming a late arrival, but I was stuck for the next five minutes. There always seems to be a stage in a cocktail party when one becomes involved in an utterly pointless conversation while everyone else seems to be discussing something of interest. Doing a bit of eariwigging while Arthur rambled on, I could hear Miles debating the prospects of a new issue with Leonard Fieldsman, who was his stockbroker as well as his bridge partner. Rhoda Penfold was having an animated conversation with Maurice's bird. Maurice himself was deep in discussion with the ancient aunt. 'We were talking about cathedrals,' he told me later, in a somewhat superior way.

Julia Lang was handing round a plate of hot sausages. At Hervey's parties you get solid refreshment, not wretched little titbits that simply take the edge off one's appetite.

'I think Klaus would be most interested in what you say about this hand,' I said to Arthur. It was a beastly trick, but it worked. Off he went.

'I could see you wanted to be rescued,' Julia remarked. We fixed up a game of tennis for the weekend; Julia is a good player, a girl champion in her youth. 'How's that scorching forehand drive of yours?' I asked her. It was a bit near the knuckle in view of her reported activities with Rhoda, but if Julia suspected any hidden meaning she gave no sign.

When Julia moved on, I joined a group who were discussing the final match at Madrid, the one that cost us the European Championship. Miles was being pompous about Rosswick's semi-collapse.

'I suppose I'm old-fashioned,' he was saying. 'I just can't understand why a young fellow should need to prop himself up with drugs; and if he does, he shouldn't be so irresponsible as to play in the last 16 boards of a vital match.'

'I don't think that's quite fair,' said Hervey. 'He told me on the way home that he was used to taking these pep pills and that normally they had no more effect than a couple of drinks. It was just bad luck that it happened to hit him at a critical moment.'

'I'm sorry, I can't accept that,' Miles persisted. 'If he was used to taking these pills he must have known the effect they were liable to have. I say again, it was thoroughly irresponsible to play in the last 16 boards of a vital match.'

Suddenly there was a deathly 'ush. Miles had raised his voice while making this pronouncement and general conversation had languished. Just at this moment Ross entered the room. He was the first to break the silence.

'Hervey, Toni, sorry I'm late. I'm off to America the day after tomorrow and I had a thousand and one things to do.' He turned to Miles and said with a smile, 'What you were saying is absolutely right, Miles. I've told myself the same thing a thousand times.'

It was smoothly done, by God. 'Well thanks, Peter, that's good of you,' said Miles in a slightly strangled voice. He laughed nervously. 'Perhaps we'd better talk about something else now.'

After a word with Hervey, Ross joined Maurice and myself, and we discussed the forthcoming tournament in Miami. When they moved on and the party began to thin out, I found myself in a corner with Helga. 'Is Frank picking you up?' I asked her. They live near me and sometimes drive me home from the club.

'No,' she said. 'He's out with a client.' Frank is a wheeler-dealer who brings the parties together when big mergers and takeover bids are planned. 'But I've got my car,' Helga added. She looked round and said quietly, 'It's parked at the end of the road, near Harrods. Wait for me there, I'll join you in a few minutes.' The bridge world is not censorious, but Frank was known to be a possessive husband even though he and Helga had frequent rows.

I made my farewells, found Helga's car, and waited for her in a convenient doorway. Oddly enough, thinking back on it, I had no presentiment as to how the evening would end. While I was waiting I thought about the conversation with Toni. Obviously she had forgotten, or forgiven, my behaviour on the last night in Madrid. I just had to find another opportunity to get her alone.

'I'm a bit pissed – you can drive, can't you?' said Helga, handing me the keys of her Alfa-Romeo. I had learned to drive an old banger along country lanes. This was a different affair and I proceeded with caution. Helga settled into a corner and closed her eyes. Either she was sleeping it off or she couldn' bear to watch my manoeuvres. As we chugged along Hyde Park she opened one eye and said, 'You know you can be prosecuted for driving too slowly as well as for driving too fast.'

When we approached my abode I thought Helga would drop me off and drive the rest of the way herself, but she said nothing, so I pressed on. She directed me to the underground garage that served her block. As I steered cautiously down the ramp she rested her hand on the inside of my thigh.

As somebody once said, in man drink arouses the appetite and dulls the performance – in woman it simply removes the inhibitions. By this time her fingers were tapping out a sensual message that needed no decoding.

'Christ, Helga,' I said, 'give it a rest until I've slotted this machine.' She said nothing, but smiled and took away her hand.

At the bottom of the lift that went up from the garage Helga stood in front of a small screen and exchanged a few words with a security officer. He released a control that opened the gates.

How the rich live. As we sailed up to the fifteenth floor I said:
'Neighbours?'
'Fuck them.'
'Frank?'
'Fuck him.'

This seemed to dispose of the immediate threats to our happiness.

The lift sighed slowly to a halt and the doors opened with a respectful silence. As Helga strode along the corridor I studied the tick-tock of her buttocks, the red dress shaping itself to each rounded cheek in turn.

'Pour a couple of brandies,' she said, drawing the curtains and making straight for the bathroom. The flat was modern — leather chairs and sofa, glass and steel tables, a large bear-rug in front of the fireplace.

On a table beside the sofa there were three photographs of Helga in riding gear. In the first two she was in the saddle, in the third she had dismounted and was stroking the animal's nose. She was standing sideways to the camera, her breasts sharply outlined, tapping her leg with a whip. The effect was very erotic.

She reappeared in a white towelling robe. 'What the hell's this?' she demanded, looking with disgust at the brandy I had poured for her. She trebled the dose. 'You're a bloody Puritan in some ways, Elvin. You don't smoke, you don't drink, probably you don't . . .'

'I do all three, as a matter of fact,' I said. 'At the moment, I know it's silly of me, but I can't help thinking that you have a husband who might return at any moment.'

'He won't be back till much later. If you're worried, I can tell the hall porter to give us a buzz. That'll give you a couple of minutes to get out of sight.'

'It's just possible that Frank might notice the second brandy glass,' I pointed out.

'My God, what a brain, no wonder you play for England. I'll tell you what I'll do. I know the people he's with, I'll ring up and find out what's happening.'

She came back from the bedroom a couple of minutes later and said:

'That was awful.'

'What was awful?'

'The wife answered the phone, as I expected. I said, was Frank ready to come home, if so I could fetch him in the car. She said, he's playing bridge, the coast is clear for a couple of hours at least, have a good time. What a reputation to have! Oh well, undress here while I wash this glass. We won't go into the bedroom. Borushka has seen a thing or two in his time,' she added, caressing the head of the bear. She turned on the fire and switched off the main light, leaving just a table lamp.

'Puritan or not, you've been looking at these photos,' she said when she came back from the kitchen. 'They're part of a set. I'll show you the others one day when I know you better.'

'You photograph well.'

'I did some modelling at one time. In fact, I first met Frank when I was showing off a fur coat for his current girl-friend. A fortnight later she had her ocelot but I had Frank.'

We were standing in front of the fire now. I drew her to me, parted her robe and moved my hands up and down her bare back. As our tongues met I grabbed her ass with both hands and pressed violently against her.

'As it's our first time we'll do it my way,' she said softly. She threw a cushion on the floor. 'There, lie on your back with your head on the cushion.'

Throwing off her robe, she lowered herself to a kneeling position, straddling my body. With her hands on the floor behind my head, she swayed from side to side, brushing her breasts against my lips and tongue. I caught each nipple between my teeth and moved my tongue round the hard point. Then I pulled her forward a little so that I could reach the back of her thighs. My hands moved slowly upwards, over and around her buttocks. She bent lower and we exchanged a long, tongue-twisting kiss. Then she sat back, her dark hair falling over her eyes, and bore gently down. All her movements were deft and practised. I had never known a woman with such an exquisite sense of timing.

While I lay panting she rolled off me and lit a cigarette. 'That wasn't bad for openers,' she remarked.

Christ, I thought, does that mean she wants an encore?

She must have caught my look because she laughed and said, 'Oh, I wasn't thinking of tonight. I was thinking that next time you could call the play, as they say in American football.'

Her next remark was unexpected:

'Toni's a sweet girl and she likes you. But basically she's not your type. She won't leave Hervey for you.'

From most women there would have been a tinge of jealousy, or at least rivalry, in such a remark, but Helga was merely stating the position as she saw it.

'What makes you think I'm so interested in Toni?' I asked.

'My dear boy!' She chuckled and blew a smoke ring.

Yes, that was a silly question.

'I suppose I'd better be pushing off,' I said.

'No hurry, my friend will ring back if there's any change in the situation. I feel like a spot of supper. What would you say to scrambled eggs and coffee?'

'Perfect.'

'Right, I won't be long.'

When she left the room I turned on the television. Some potty psychiatrist was saying that yes, there might possibly be a connection between arson, bombing, mugging, kidnapping, rape, riots, as depicted on television, and arson, bombing, mugging, kidnapping, rape, riots, such as occurred in real life; there was much research to be done, for which money would be needed.

Bloody idiot! Isn't it plain to everyone except psychiatrists and the BBC that all such activities thrive on the publicity given to them? Where I live, we have the additional nuisance of squatters on the top floor. They have various unpleasant habits and we have to bribe the postman to deliver parcels individually.

Helga returned with two trays and I turned off the set. We talked about the scene at the party when Miles dropped his brick. 'The way Ross let Miles off the hook was really something,' Helga remarked. 'He's a sweet boy.'

'His sex life is a mystery to me. What goes on, do you think?'

'If you mean, has he made a play for me, the answer's no. Ross is the same charmer towards young and old, pretty and plain. I can only suppose he's waiting for the right girl.' Then Helga referred to the incident at the club: 'You were there when Frank had that row with Mosey, weren't you?'

'Yes,' I said. 'It was very amusing.'

'Well, that little prick Mosey wrote to the committee the same evening, complaining that Frank had thrown away a game to spite him. I don't know what happened exactly, but Frank admitted he was in the wrong and in the end he sent Mosey a cheque with a brief note.

'Frank's a vengeful sod,' she went on. 'Leonard Fieldsman was here a night or two ago and they were talking about Mosey. I think they've got some plan to shop him over a share deal. Something to do with manipulating a share that Mosey has been plugging. At least, that's the general idea. If you know which way a share's likely to go, whether up or down, you can make a profit. Would you like me to find out more about it?'

I told her that at the moment I'd be damned glad of any opportunity to turn an honest penny, or even a dishonest one. I usually keep my financial troubles to myself, but Helga's not the sort of person with whom you have to pretend.

When I left, she told me to take the lift at the end of the corridor. 'Then the hall porter won't know where you've come from.'

It had been an enjoyable evening, but walking home I felt depressed. Helga was probably right about Toni; she herself was more my type. *Post coitum tristis*, as the man said. I go along with that.

Miami

by Maurice Levine

'We meet in the solicitor's office at 10.30 on Wednesday morning,' I told Elvin over the phone. 'That's the day before we leave. You've got the address. Can you make it on your own, do you think?' I had made all the travel arrangements for our trip to Miami and practically taken him by the hand to the American Embassy. I was bored with acting as his nursemaid.

The reason for the meeting was to sign the Agreement between Habib and ourselves. We had been sent a draft copy. Most of it was okay, but I intended to raise a point about the payment of win bonuses.

When I got to the office on Wednesday Habib was already there but not, of course, Elvin. A young girl in a tight red sweater showed us into the office of Mr William Harbottle, senior partner of Harbottle, Crabbe, Wilkinson, and Harbottle. After the introductions Shoukry asked me to look at paragraph 23, section 4(c) of the draft Agreement. While I was reading this there was a sharp yelp from the doorway and Elvin breezed in.

'What's this, the Atlantic Charter?' was his first remark when handed the document.

'Cross the t's and dot the i's, that's what we're here for,' said Harbottle amiably. 'No sense in leaving loose ends, is there?' He peered at each of us in turn over his spectacles, as though we were all expected to answer. 'Well now, I believe that you, Mr Habib, and you, Mr Levine, have read this draft, which has been prepared according to your instructions. Any small changes can be incorporated and initialled. Subject to that, final copies are ready for your signatures and the business can be completed this morning. If it meets with your approval, that is.'

Habib nodded and turned to Elvin. 'I was just asking Maurice to look at paragraph 23, section 4(c), on page 19,' he said. 'You see how it reads: "When entry is made for a team event five players shall always be nominated on the entry form. Mr E. Starr, Mr M. Levine and Mr S. Habib, captain, shall be permanent members of the team, available to play whenever required".'

'Unfortunately,' Habib went on, 'because of my other commitments I may not always be available. As you know, I am unable to travel with you to America tomorrow. Some alteration in this clause is therefore needed.'

I knew Elvin would think it very funny that Habib should apologize for not being able to play. Before he could make one of his tactless comments I said:

'Even if you can't be there, Shoukry, you can be entered on the form as captain. After "permanent members of the team" we could add "it being understood that Mr Habib may not always be available to play".'

'That would appear to cover the point,' said Harbottle. 'Do all you gentlemen agree? Very good, let me get that down. Now, is there any other point that any of you wishes to raise?'

'Could we turn to paragraph 26 on page 21?' I asked. 'It says that win bonuses would be included in the retainer, which is to be paid quarterly. If we won a couple of events early on, we would have to wait three months for the bonus of £500 each. Could we make it instead, "such bonuses to be paid within fourteen days of the event"?'

'If you wish,' said Habib.

'... within fourteen days ...' murmured Harbottle, making a note of the change. He rang a little bell. 'Ah, Miriam, we have two small changes. Would you be so kind as to enter them on all three copies of the final Agreement and bring them back to us? Thank you.'

Elvin, who was facing the door, gave Miriam a big wink. She ignored him, I was pleased to see. While we were waiting Elvin asked whether there was anything in the Agreement about publication rights.

'I certainly hope that my notes on the Habibi Heart will be put into book form before very long,' said Shoukry. 'But forgive me, I don't see quite how this concerns you, Elvin.'

'Maurice and I are going to play the system for the next six months at least. If we do well and it catches on, do we get a share of the profits from books, teaching manuals, franchises, and what not?'

Why didn't I think of that? A *goy* giving me lessons in business — I must be slipping. Habib said it was too late to incorporate any of this in the Agreement but he was willing to discuss it later.

The girl returned with the bumf, we initialled the changes and added our signatures. Old Harbottle produced some sherry and Habib made a performance of presenting each of us with a cheque for £1,000, the signing-on fee which I had negotiated.

On the way back in the car Habib remarked that he would be following our fortunes in America.

'What a shame you won't be there to play yourself,' said Elvin, bold as brass.

'Alas, duty calls,' the Arab replied.

He dropped us off at Marble Arch and wished us luck. As the car drove off, I said to Elvin:

'I wouldn't try to be a *hochim* with Shoukry if I were you. He's not a fool.'

'He is if he thinks we're going to let him play when there's a £500 bonus at stake,' Elvin answered. 'But he's not blind. Do you think his beady black eyes didn't notice you ogling Rosanna at the Dorchester the other day? Disgusting, I call it.'

I had done much better with Rosanna than Elvin with the skinny girl at the solicitor's office. One day when I phoned, Habib wasn't in and I had a long natter with Rosanna. I didn't answer Elvin's remark.

I had told Elvin when to meet me at the terminal, and he was only six minutes late, not bad for him. 'Here I am in the nicotine,' he said, laden with luggage and, if you please, *two* tennis rackets. Actually we were in fairly good time. After checking in, we had a coffee and went to the bookstall.

'Are you looking for *Son of the Bride of the Beast*?' Elvin asked me, rolling about with laughter.

How stupid can you get! It was true that on the way back from Madrid I had read a book with a title something like that, but you don't get much choice of English books at a Spanish airport.

On the plane we discussed Habib's system. Elvin was unhappy about certain parts.

'We're stuck with it, you'd better get used to that,' I said. 'However, I agree that the two-way bids are too dangerous as they stand.' I suggested a small but vital change.

Elvin kept on about the forcing pass on strong hands. 'Good opponents will trap us,' he insisted. 'We could go for 1,100, not even saving a slam.'

This was true. The Arab had underestimated the risk, because he wasn't used to playing against top-class opposition.

Elvin soon wearied of the technical discussion and began asking me about the financial arrangements for the trip — had Habib advanced enough to cover the entry fees, that sort of thing. He tried to be casual about it, but he was obviously skint even though we had just had the advance. Elvin doesn't seem to realize that his scrapes are common knowledge. Frank Rowlands summed him up quite cleverly: 'Elvin borrows from Peter to pay Paul, then from Paul to repay Peter.' Frank also told me that Elvin wasn't half so clever at poker as he thought he was.

For the rest of the journey I settled down to Heather Bollard's latest, *The Virgin and the Gorilla*. At Miami airport there was a large banner saying 'Light and Rest Your Saddle'. An immigration officer asked us the purpose of our visit. 'To lift one of your pewter cups and a few thousand dollars,' Elvin replied. It's always stupid to take the piss out of an official in uniform, anybody knows that. I butted in quickly to save the man from being annoyed. Then we moved to customs. The official there said in a nasal tone. 'Wotugotin that bag, man?' I was so flummoxed by the peculiar accent that I just gaped at him. 'Okay, toinitout,' said the man. I hate anyone rummaging among my personal belongings in public. Elvin chose to be on his best behaviour now and wasn't held up at all.

The airport bus dropped us at our hotel, the Sun Palace, looking on to the beach and dazzlingly white. Entering the lobby, I had my first view of a speciality we had been told about, the 'hospitality desk'. The tournament was sponsored by the Florida Citrus Fruits Board and there were desks with pretty girls in costumes representing oranges, lemons and grapefruit. We gave our names, paid our dues, and were presented with a load of brochures and programmes.

Further on there was a fourth desk, with a placard saying 'Lonely Hearts Bureau'. There was an older woman behind the desk, in more conventional attire. 'Are you doubles or singles?' she asked.

'This is what I call service,' said Elvin. 'Despite my affection for my small friend here, I wish to be classified as a single. My favourite type is . . .'

'Take no notice of my friend,' I said hastily. 'We expect to play together in all events.'

'So you won't be wanting partners, right?' She shifted her gum. 'I'll still take down your names, though. Limey humour,' she called to the girls as we moved on.

There was a mountain of fruit in my room and a friendly note from Ross. The bedroom was very ordinary, compared to the luxury of the public rooms. When I had unpacked and changed, I looked through the bumf the girls had given us. Rule 9 stated: *Courtesy to partner and opponents will be strictly enforced.* This I couldn't wait to see!

The telephone rang; it was Ross. 'Hi, welcome to the old USA,' he said. 'I wanted to meet you at the airport but I got dragged into a practice match. Mustn't let you down, what? The boys here would split themselves to hear me talking like that. Everybody's dying to meet you. Come down to the bar as soon as you're ready.'

I knocked on Elvin's door and gave him the message. I could see he didn't approve of the open shirt and loose sweater I was wearing. 'I thought this was a place for casual wear,' I said. 'We might be going somewhere for dinner,' he replied. So I went back to my room and put on my blue velour jacket, a vermillion bow tie, and corduroy trousers.

There were wild whoops when we entered the bar. Ross's partner, Rhett Brindley, had fair wavy hair, pale blue eyes and good teeth. His face was red from the sun. He was dressed like a hippie, with jeans, a blue shirt open to the waist, and a necklace of sea shells. I'd have been all right in my sweater after all.

'Pete's been telling us about this crazy system of yours,' Brindley said, after Ross had introduced us to all his friends. 'A forcing pass in first or second – gee, that'll create waves. Habibi Heart, it's a great name for a cocktail, eh, Joe? What'll it be, boys?'

There was a burst of laughter when I asked for a tomato juice.

'Prohibition's over, fella!' one of Rhett's friends called out. I like good wine, but you wouldn't get anything worth drinking here. Ross pressed Elvin to sample a Daiquiri.

Rhett invited Ross, Elvin and myself to have dinner with him at a Polynesian restaurant called the Waikiki. The food on the aeroplane had been as dreary as usual and I was more than ready for some nosh, but a stop-off for 'Grog in the Pirates Lair' was evidently a must. Rhett tried to slip me a mixture in a scooped-out coconut, saying it was non-alcoholic, but I could smell the rum. Elvin drank two of them and was so knocked out that for once he had nothing to say.

During dinner Brindley gave us a run-down on the leading personalities in American bridge. He also described the 'payola system'. All the top teams, it appeared, were financed by some rich man who paid the expenses and sometimes played himself. If a top star was invited to join a team his first question, according to Rhett, was 'Who picks up the tab?' Elvin asked if there was a transfer system, as in football.

A big heavy-featured man with a coloured girl on his arm came into the restaurant and nodded to Brindley. 'That's Jim

Roper,' said Rhett. 'I can tell you an amusing story about him. Last week there was a big backgammon tournament here. Jim's no slouch at bridge and a top pro at backgammon. In an early round he played against a cocky young bridge bum from out west, who threw good dice and got to 12 all, in a match to 13. Now Jim made his opponent a proposition: "Even if you get through this round you haven't got much chance of finishing in the big money. Let me win and you can have twenty per cent of my action." The youngster said okay, but when they restarted he continued to throw luckily, saw that he had the game won, and suddenly declared "No deal!" So Jim was knocked out, but believe it or not he had the nerve to protest the result. The committee just told them to replay the last game. Can you beat it?'

'Didn't anyone raise a stink?' I asked.

'Raise a stink?' said Brindley, mimicking an English accent. 'That's cute! Roper lost in the next round, so nobody bothered.'

Ross wanted Elvin and me to join him at a party later, but it was already midnight and we were tired from the journey and change of time.

The first event in the bridge the next day was a two-session Charity Pairs. 'You two must have a great chance in this,' Brindley informed us. 'The pros usually split up. Ross has a punter lined up and I'm playing with my wife, heaven help me. There won't be any strong pairs around and nobody will understand your system. I'll see if I can get a price from Larry Summers.'

He came back in a few minutes, well pleased with himself. 'Larry had you at 20/1,' he said, 'but he wouldn't take more than $100. Said his book didn't justify it. Do you want half?' I asked for $10 and Elvin took the rest.

We had a good session. 'You're lying third,' Rhett told us over a maple-nut sundae in the coffee-shop. 'The pairs ahead of you are nothing. Ross and his punter are eighth. In case you're worried, Jennifer and I are poised at 163rd.'

We had another big session in the evening and won by a clear top. Rhett reported that Larry had lost money on his book and was furious. He was telling anyone who would listen that we ought not to have been allowed to play together or play an unknown system.

In the next event, the open pairs, the rules were more strict and Elvin and I weren't allowed to play the Habibi Heart. We muddled along with a makeshift one club system and were never in the hunt. Our best set was against a leading player called Danny Luten, playing with a tubby little man who was evidently a punter. Luten yelled at him after every board and I thought of Rule 9, *Courtesy to partner and opponents will be strictly enforced*. At the end of the round Luten muttered something about wasting his time with an utter idiot and went off to what they call the juice box, which dispenses fresh orange juice. Elvin followed him and the tubby little man said to me:

'Am I right in thinking, sir, that you are Mr Ell-vine Starr, of London, England?'

'No, that's my partner. I'm Maurice Levine.'

'Allow me to introduce myself, Mr Levine. I am Horace L. Carter, Jr, from Dayton, Ohio. You may not have guessed it, but I'm paying Dan Luten $1,000 to play with me in this tournament. I guess if it were only $500 he'd have kicked me in the balls by now.'

When he saw we weren't going to finish in the top ten Elvin began chatting up the mini-skirted caddies who moved the boards from table to table. In the end we finished 30th. Ross and Brindley were third.

We had a free day before the main event, the Citrus Bowl for teams of four, and Brindley invited us to his home. Ross had told me that Rhett was a 'bean merchant', in Elvin's phrase. He had a fine house, with a tennis court and swimming pool. His wife, Jennifer, was a pleasant girl but no looker. It occurred to me that the money was probably hers.

After lunch Ross began a game of gin rummy with Jennifer and one of the guests, while Elvin and Rhett played tennis. They appeared to be about equal in the knock-up and settled on a stake for the best of every five games. I had seen Elvin play before and I knew he was stringing Brindley along. He was about $500 in front when a high wind blew up and they had to

stop. While we were having drinks in the sun parlour Rhett said:
'Larry Summers is giving a party on his yacht and I promised him we'd look in.'

'On a boat, in this wind!' I said, horrified. I am easily seasick.

'Oh, Maurice, don't worry, the bay is sheltered,' Ross assured me. 'And it's not a tornado, exactly.'

The four of us drove off to the party in Brindley's car. The yacht turned out to be a dirty-looking tub, bobbing up and down amid some other dilapidated vessels. We walked along a rickety plank to the deck and Brindley led the way to a dimly-lit saloon, where half-a-dozen men and a couple of females were lying around in various states of undress. Larry greeted us coolly and made single-word introductions to Hank, Val, Sidney, Rube and so forth. Elvin looked around in disgust, while Ross quickly found a place for himself and accepted a joint from his neighbour.

I had been to pot parties at university and knew it was simple enough to pretend to puff away. I chose a dark corner and tried to be inconspicuous. Elvin sat opposite, folding his arms and ignoring the joints that were being passed around.

The conversation was as stupid and pretentious as it usually is on these occasions:

'Gee, he got into my brain, man.'

'His sensitivity was fantastic, as though he was oblivious to the world of mammon.'

'He had the peace and purity of a flower.'

In the silence that followed this last remark Elvin called across:

'I wonder whether anyone thinks of you as a little snowdrop, Maurice.'

Rhett said sharply, 'Cut it out, Elvin.'

There was silence for a minute or two, then Elvin spoke up again:

'Hi, beautiful! I'm not talking to you now, Maurice. I'm talking to Val.'

Val was the less unprepossessing of the two scrubbers, a pallid blonde with streaky hair that might have been quite pretty if it were washed. She was wearing patched jeans and a T-shirt, wide open down the front.

'It seems we have an unappreciative guest,' said Larry in an unpleasant tone. 'Val is stoned at the moment. When she's not stoned she's Hank's girl.'

Hank lumbered to his feet and said, 'Piss off, you lousy limey bum, before I take you apart.'

Elvin laughed and stood up, facing him. Hank was four inches taller, but I had heard a story of Elvin half-killing a youth who tried to mug him. Before anything could happen Rhett jumped up and said:

'Cool it, both of you. Elvin, I'll drive you back to the hotel. Coming, Maurice? 'Bye, Larry, see you tomorrow.'

'What a shower!' said Elvin loudly, as we walked off. As soon as we were in the car Brindley turned on Elvin:

'That wasn't smart, you know. Larry runs a big operation in these parts and Hank has plenty of pull, too.'

'Why the hell didn't you tell me it was a pot party?' Elvin replied. 'I wouldn't have gone.'

'It wasn't a pot party, it was just a party where a few people smoke pot. Half-a-dozen like it go on every night at the hotel. Larry has to be a bit careful, and the boat is safer.'

'I'm learning,' said Elvin savagely. 'And another thing: why did you let Ross stay on? What sort of state will he be in tomorrow?'

'He's used to it. He'll be okay.'

'He seemed at home. I noticed that.'

Elvin could be a very embarrassing companion at times and surprisingly intolerant as well, considering his own character. I didn't care much for Brindley myself, but it was silly to rub him up the wrong way. It was a shock to see Ross hobnobbing with those people on the boat, but again it was none of our business.

Whether or not Ross had a hangover, he and Brindley had a poor match in the first round of the teams. We had a narrow squeak against four college boys, who played surprisingly well. After that it was plain sailing till the quarter-final, where we met a team containing the backgammon expert, Jim Roper. Brindley uttered dark warnings to 'watch out'.

Elvin and I had a disastrous set in the third quarter, entirely our own fault. When we compared scores at the interval, Brindley was insufferably rude. 'Je-sus,' he kept on saying as one dismal result followed another. 'This is simply ridiculous. We'll have to break up you two. No more Habibi Heart.'

I thought Elvin would explode, but the onslaught seemed to amuse him. 'Did Maurice and I say anything when you and Ross played like cunts in the first round?' he asked. 'So we're a few points down. We'll continue as we are.' We won in the end and all was forgiven.

Rhett arrived before midday the next morning to give Elvin and me a run-down on our opponents in the semi-final, a team he distrusted. One pair was known as 'Exchange Telegraph', he informed us. The other employed 'angelisti', which I took to be an Italian word meaning 'messengers'. 'I'm not going to let Ventura's girlfriend sit opposite him and give him the wig-wags,' Rhett declared.

Elvin was bored by this talk. 'I don't care if they've got electronic bugs up their asses,' he said. 'Just play decent bridge and we won't lose.'

We were sitting on the terrace and I heard my name called on the loud-speaker. I went to the porter's desk and came back with a cable that read:

CONGRATULATIONS VICTORIOUS PROGRESS STOP ASSUME YOU HAVE QUALIFIED FOR SEMIFINAL STOP I LOOK FORWARD TO HEARING FULL ACCOUNT STOP HAVE ALTERED ENGAGEMENTS AND BOOKED PLANE DUE TO ARRIVE MIDDAY THURSDAY STOP HABIBI HEART WILL CARRY US TO VICTORY STOP WILL BE WITH YOU SOON MY GOOD FRIENDS STOP SHOUKRY HABIB

'Doesn't economize when he sends a cable, does he?' Elvin remarked. 'Today's Thursday, isn't it?'

Ross had joined us now. He told us over lunch to disregard Brindley's suspicions. 'He's paranoiac.'

When Elvin and I sat down in the open room to play against Ventura and his partner, I noticed that the dark girl attached to Ventura was sitting behind him and not opposite. We were discussing systems when there was a commotion in the doorway and in came the Arab.

'You haven't started?' he said anxiously. 'Then I'm just in time. Maurice, how are you? Elvin, I trust I find you well. Now, what is our best line-up? Do I play with you, Maurice, or with Elvin?'

Elvin was completely 'discombobulated', to use one of his own silly words. After a moment I said:

'Shoukry, it's wonderful to see you. But I think I ought to tell you that we have made a special study of the system our opponents are playing. You might be at a disadvantage.'

'Oh, no,' said Habib, showing his white teeth in an expansive smile. 'This won't be the first time I have played against American opponents. Besides, a captain must sail his own ship, isn't that so? Well now, Maurice, I expect you are a little more secure in the system than Elvin, so I will play the first quarter with you.'

Elvin now found his tongue:

'Unfortunately, we've given our line-up to the opposing captain,' he said. 'We're not allowed to change now.'

'Oh, that's quite all right,' said Ventura. 'There will be no objection from us.'

'That's remarkably handsome of you,' said Elvin, rising from his chair. 'Carry on, *mon capitaine*.' He left the room.

The game with Habib went quite well, to my relief. I thought we had at least held our own. When we finished we left a message for the other pair to join us in Habib's suite. While Shoukry was calling room service the door from the bedroom opened and in came Shoukry's friend, Rosanna. She looked ravishing in white jeans and an apple-green tunic. Elvin waved to her with a casual 'Hi, O stealer of men's hearts'. I stood up, kissed her hand, and said, 'Shoukry didn't tell us you were here too, Miss Mamarbachi. What a delightful surprise!' I had found out her name from the receptionist at the Dorchester. Women appreciate that sort of thing.

Brindley and Ross came up a minute or two later. They didn't know that Habib had been playing. I dare say they were relieved to find we were a few points in front.

Habib began the next set with Elvin, playing in the closed room. I looked in at the other semi-final for a while, but the play was very slow and after watching a couple of hands I went outside to the pool, wearing the large Mexican hat I had purchased at the airport. Rosanna was lying on one of the mattresses, a vision in a white bikini that set off her brown skin. She put down the magazine she was reading and beckoned me over.

I'm on the small side and even my momma never called me handsome. I play tournament bridge because being an international player gives me standing with the girls. But was I going to have to work now! Rosanna was beautiful, I was not; she was Egyptian, I was Jewish.

My first move always is to find a common interest. I had a stroke of luck early on. I made a comment on the tunic she had been wearing earlier and it turned out that her father had been the manager in a fabric factory. Textile design had been one of my subjects at university and we talked about materials. After a while a breeze blew up. I helped her to collect her things and we went into the hotel by a side entrance. 'Your hat is sweet but rather conspicious,' she said, meaning conspicuous. Still talking, we entered her room together.

I asked her about her family and how she had first met Habib. They were both Copts. It was quite common, apparently, for the girls to be given French or Italian names. Sitting on a couch by the window, I told her how beautiful she was but didn't try to touch her.

I found she wasn't in the least in awe of Habib. 'He rushes round the world making money, but he doesn't know what he really wants. He has girls everywhere, like a sailorman.'

'Does he expect you to be faithful?'

'*Qui va à la chasse perd sa place*,' she answered, translating neatly: Who goes on the chase loses his place. 'He's jealous though,' she added. 'Very possessing.'

'Is he a good lover?'

She laughed. 'He's like all men. He pleases himself.'

'Not like all men. Have you ever had a Jewish lover?'

'No-o . . . but I've always half wanted one.'

'You've got one.'

We moved into the bedroom. Ten minutes later I was just bringing her to a pitch of excitement when there was a knock on the door from the corridor.

'*Mon Dieu*,' said Rosanna, 'that must be Shoukry. I put out the Do Not Disturb notice, none of the servants would dare to knock.'

'But Shoukry's playing downstairs,' I said, in a panic.

'He could have come up for something. Quickly, hide.'

I rushed towards the wardrobe, but Rosanna said 'No, he might want something from his jacket, get under the bed.'

She put on a robe and went to the door. I could hear them talking in French. Rosanna said she had a *mal de tête* from the journey and was lying down. Shoukry wanted his hay-fever pills. She fetched them from the bathroom and after a few moments Shoukry left. I crawled out, my heart beating.

I was relieved that Rosanna had not thought of resuming after this alarm. We dressed quickly and went back to the sitting-room.

'My God, you left your glasses on the table,' Rosanna exclaimed. 'I hope . . .'

'Wouldn't he have said something if he'd noticed them?'

'I don't know. He's deviant. No, devious. You'd better go now.'

Elvin and Habib had done well and we now led by 20 match points. Habib took us all to dinner in the roof-garden restaurant. To my great relief there didn't seem to be any change in his attitude towards me. He said he had to make some telephone calls and suggested that Elvin and I play the next quarter.

We had one or two unlucky boards in this session and our lead was cut. It was vital that Elvin and I should play on, but clearly this was not Habib's intention. Ross, Elvin and I managed to get a private word together. Elvin was frantic:

'If we win this event the bonus is a thousand quid, is that right?'

'Yes.' This was the bonus for premier events not carrying a cash prize.

'Then for Christ's sake stop the Arab from playing. You tell him, Ross.'

'Why elect me?'

It was too late anyway. Habib descended on us and said:

'I enjoyed our session, Elvin, and I think you and I should play now. You don't mind, Maurice?'

I was glad to be out of it. I watched them play for a while in the open room. They started reasonably well, but then disaster struck. Elvin and I had reorganized the opening two-bids and Elvin forgot that Habib's method was different. They had a very expensive misunderstanding. Nothing went right after that and we lost the match by a small margin.

Shoukry was disappointed but felt the system had justified itself. 'Let's go up to my room and drown our sorrows,' said Brindley, more amiable than I had expected. It struck me that he probably wanted to make a good impression on Habib. We took the lift skywards to Brindley's magnificent penthouse overlooking the bay. While we were discussing some hands from the final session, the telephone rang. Brindley spoke quietly for a few moments, then put down the receiver and said:

'That was Larry Summers. He has some friends in and is thinking of a poker game. Ross will play, I know. What about you, Shoukry, do you play poker?'

'Not well, I'm afraid,' said Habib. 'But it would give me great pleasure to join your game.'

'What sort of stakes?' asked Elvin.

'Just a friendly game,' said Rhett. 'We normally start with a stack of $500 and open the pots for 20.'

This suited Elvin, who had won over $1,000 while he had been over here. I said I would like to kibitz for a while. My momma plays poker every day of her life, so I know the game, but I'd rather watch than play, especially for these stakes. At poker money's the name of the game, and money's always interesting.

Rhett asked Habib if there was any chance of Rosanna joining us. 'She doesn't play but if she's not asleep I'll ask her to come up,' Shoukry replied. 'Must have an attendant moll to pass round the fire-water,' commented Elvin brightly.

Larry's suite was almost as grand as Rhett's. There were two people with him when he arrived, both bridge players whom I knew slightly. Rosanna appeared about twenty minutes later. After she had helped to serve drinks and sandwiches I tried to lure her to the balcony, but she shook her head, with a warning glance at Habib.

The game began quietly, mostly jackpots or five-card stud. I noticed that Habib, although the money could have meant nothing to him, played a very conservative game. Elvin, as one would expect, was much more flashy. At one point he opened a jackpot, bought one card, and checked. There was a double and a see, then Elvin redoubled. There was one drop, one see, and Elvin produced a full house. This successful sandbag, a common enough manoeuvre, gave him great satisfaction. He was holding good cards and won about $400 in the first half hour. Ross was winning, too, but in such a diffident, almost apologetic, way that one scarcely noticed it.

After a time the game shifted to dealer's choice. Some of the choices were way out. In this type of game it's essential to play tight, because the odds are unfamiliar and often deceptive. Elvin's winnings soon began to dribble away. He had lost his profit, his original $500, and half his second $500 when a round of seven-card high-low was suggested.

In seven-card stud a player who stays in the pot till the finish receives two cards face down, four face up, and one face down. High-low means that the pot is divided between the best hand and the worst hand (the best misère, that is). The initial ante was only $5, but with four betting intervals such pots can run very high.

In one pot where Elvin stayed to the finish his four cards showing on the table were 2 J 7 10. It was clear from the tempo of his betting that he was aiming for a low hand. He had raised after his fifth card, the 7, and as two 7s had already been seen there was no possibility that he had 7-7 in the hole. Good players notice that sort of thing. Of the two opponents still in the pot, one was obviously aiming high, the other low. Elvin was now caught in a typical squeeze. The player who was going high was confident of winning his half of the pot, and the third player could see that Elvin, at best, might have a 7 5 misère. That's a pretty good hand, but an opponent who is 6 high or 7 4 has a cinch – he knows he must win. Elvin stayed for one round too long before he realized he was beaten. When he called the final bet he put in an IOU for $800.

The two Americans who were dividing the pot raised their eyebrows and glanced at Larry, the host.

'We play for cash here,' said Larry. 'Not peanuts or bits of paper.'

'I'm sorry about that,' said Elvin tightly. 'Perhaps you'd like me to swim home? I can give the money to any friend of yours in England. Alternatively, I'll be over for the Cavendish Club Pairs early next year and I'll bring the cash then.'

There was an awkward pause. Larry, who held the cards, riffled the pack but did not begin the next deal. I thought Habib would intervene, but it was Ross who came to the rescue: 'No need to go through that performance, Elvin,' he said. 'I'll settle for you now, you can pay me back later.'

'Thank you,' said Elvin, not very warmly. 'I'll write you a note.'

The game broke up after this round. Elvin, Ross and I ended the evening in Habib's suite. Elvin's temper was not improved when Shoukry read him a little lecture:

'If you will forgive me for saying so, Elvin, you stayed too long in that last pot. I was sure you were beaten when you ran into the first double. And you know, it's not wise to play for more money that you have in your pocket. I can tell you a little story about that. I was a lad of nineteen at the time, studying at Cairo university, and . . .'

But my eyes were on Rosanna and I didn't listen to Shoukry's story.

As we had been knocked out of the main event, we had

a free day before returning to England. Habib decided to play in the open pairs with Ross. I tried to make a date with Rosanna for the afternoon, but it was impossible as everything was fixed for her to go to a fashion show. 'They're showing the spring collection. All the big shoots will be there and Shoukry will want to know all about it. He has an interest in the firm.'

Elvin assumed I would be at his disposal. 'Will Habib lend us his jam jar?'

'His . . . oh, yes, he said I could borrow it any time?'

'We might go to the races.'

Racing bores me stiff. 'What about this Jai-Alai they've been advertising?' I asked. 'You can bet on that too.'

'Can you? I didn't know that. Have you any idea how to get there? What's Brindley doing?'

'He plans to go deep-sea fishing, he told me.'

'Pah!'

'What do you mean, pah?'

'I mean it's a loathsome pursuit.'

'You think fishing is wrong?'

'The general assumption that animals have no basic right to a peaceful existence is certainly wrong. To mangle and kill splendid creatures like sharks and whales is cruel and disgusting beyond belief.'

'You went to a bullfight in Madrid, I seem to remember.'

'I don't hold with that, either. Since you mention it, I didn't go to the bullfight to watch the bullfight. I had a different objective that evening.'

'Did you explain that to the bull?'

'I say, Maurice, that's not at all bad. If you play with me a little longer you'll acquire a gift for repartee.'

The drive to the Jai-Alai took half an hour. The game is derived from pelota and the players had unpronounceable Basque names. They bounded about like mad, at one moment retrieving a low ball in their basket-like scoops, at the next leaping into the air like Nijinsky to make a dramatic volley.

Elvin was fascinated by the betting. The court had three walls, with a net at one side. The bookmakers stood behind the net, in a sort of orchestra pit, and the spectators, sitting in the balcony above, made their bets by throwing down tennis balls containing their selections and the money. The bookies made a note of the instructions and threw back the tennis ball with a receipt.

At the bar in the interval, who should we see but Larry, Hank, and the girl, Val, cleaned up and looking almost presentable. 'Well, if if isn't Percy the Pot Peddler,' Elvin called out. Hank clenched his fists, but Larry spoke a word to him and he nodded. Soon we were separated from them in the crowd.

When we left at the end of the game I went towards the car to unlock it, then noticed that Elvin wasn't with me. He had started an altercation with Larry and Hank. As I went to drag him away, a cop appeared and told them to break it up. Elvin strode back to our car in front of me and got into the driver's seat, forgetting it was a left-hand drive. I saw Hank go into a phone-booth.

I dropped Elvin at the entrance to the Sun Palace and, as requested by Habib, delivered the car to Lot 473. These underground garages are cold, eerie places, dimly lit. As I turned a corner into a new bay, on my way back to the entrance, the overhead light went off. At first it was as black as Rabbi Benji's hat. As my eyes grew more accustomed I saw shadows ahead and heard a sound of scuffling feet. I had a sense of alarm.

'Is anyone there?' I called out.

There was a clanging sound, like a metal rod striking a railing, or perhaps a car bumper.

'I can't see. Is anyone there?' I called again.

There was silence for a few moments, then from the left I heard, or imagined I heard, a deep voice intoning 'Fee Fi Fo Fum', and from the right, 'I smell the blood of an Englishman.'

Thoroughly alarmed now, I started to walk towards the attendant's hut, a dim yellow light in the distance. As I passed the next car a torch suddenly shone in my eyes and at the same moment I felt a violent blow on the back of my neck. I stumbled and fell, my glasses flew off, and as I tried to get up a flailing fist struck me in the eye and another blow knocked me to the ground. I was kicked in the ribs from both sides and one of the men – there must have been two – stamped on my hand. I heard a car door slam nearby and the men ran off. It was all over in twenty seconds.

I called for help, but no one answered. I groped for my glasses and found the frames, but one of the lenses was out and the other was shattered. Slowly and painfully, supporting myself on the cars I passed, I dragged my way to the pool of light ahead.

The attendant, a thin old man with tired eyes, did not seem greatly surprised by my appearance. He gave me a chair and offered me a drink. 'Want me to call the cops?' he asked. No, I thought, that would mean inquiries and delays, and we were due to leave the next morning. 'If you could just get me the key to my room,' I said. He made a couple of calls on a wall phone, and in time a black boy appeared with my key. He took me to the lift and helped me to my room. As I felt in my pocket for some money, it struck me as surprising that I had not been robbed.

I bathed my eye, which was bleeding, and lay on my bed, feeling sick. My ribs were very sore, but so far as I could tell nothing was broken. After about ten minutes there was a knock at the door. Before I could answer, the door was opened from outside. It was a burly man with grizzled hair, who constantly worried an unlit cigar.

'You Mr Levine? I'm the house 'tec, name of Potter. You okay to tell me what happened? Everything you can remember.'

'I ought to inform the cops,' he said when I finished my story. 'Not that they'd do anything. Happens too often.'

'I had my wallet with me,' I said. 'Isn't it odd that I wasn't robbed?'

'Nope. You say you heard a car door slam, they may have been scared off. Anyway, there's plenty of young hooligans around here who'd knock a honky about for kicks.'

'I didn't say they were blacks. I couldn't see them. And not many blacks would know that Fee Fi Fo Fum business, would they?'

'You want a doctor?' he asked, not commenting on this.

'Won't cost you nothing. Hotel's insured for injuries to guests on the premises.'

Doctors could mean delays, too. 'No, thank you,' I said. 'We're leaving tomorrow and I'll be all right. But my glasses are broken, as I told you. I have a reserve pair, but they're out of date and I'll have to have new lenses made up when I get back to England. Will the insurance cover that?'

'Don't know about that,' he said, transferring the chewed cigar from one side of his mouth to the other. 'Have to read the small print.' He chuckled briefly. 'But then, if you've lost your glasses you won't be able to read the small print, will you?'

London and York

by Elvin Starr

On our last morning in Miami I was standing at the bottom of the hotel steps, organizing the luggage, when a strange sight appeared through the swing doors. It was Maurice, wearing his Mexican sun hat, fully a yard wide. The braggadocio effect was enhanced by a piratical eye-patch.

'*Buenos dias, Sancho*,' I said. '*Que te he pasado*? Don't tell me: the other fellow's in hospital.'

Without removing his headgear Maurice manœuvred himself crabwise into the back seat of the taxi. 'I was mugged,' he said. 'Peculiar business. I'll tell you about it later. Where are the others?'

'Habib and your Egyptian piece left earlier for Paris. He says he may be back in England for the trials. At least he can't play in those.'

'Don't blame Shoukry,' said Maurice grumpily. 'It was you who forgot the system.'

Personally I thought it was Maurice's fault we lost the semi-final. He should have reminded me, before I played with Habib, that we had made some changes in the system.

I had enjoyed the American trip in most ways. On the plus side, I was satisfied that with a little more practice Maurice and I would be a very formidable partnership. To our susprise, we had found that Shoukry was a competent player who wouldn't let us down. On the minus side, my financial position was worse than ever, because now I owed Ross from the poker game.

Two days after we got back to London I woke up with the

feeling that something was wrong. It was. The doorbell was ringing with a special note of urgency. The bell was reinforced by a loud knock. I threw on a dressing-gown and opened the door to reveal an unremarkable member of society carrying a bowler hat.

'Mr Starr?'

'Yes.'

'I have to inform you, sir, that I am here in connection with a judgment summons against you.' He handed me a document. 'May I come in?'

I glanced at the document. 'But this is for my brother, Elvin. I'm Martin Starr.'

Odd Job stroked his chin reflectively.

'Mr Elvin Starr's brother, eh? But this is Mr Elvin Starr's apartment? His furniture?'

'Yes, it's his flat. He's lent it to me for a while. I don't know about the furniture. It probably belongs to the landlord.'

Odd Job was looking round. 'That Georgian desk must be worth a few bob. Not the sort of thing I'd expect a landlord to provide.'

'Ah, that's a family piece. It belongs to my mother, Lady Frances Starr.'

'Hm. And where is Mr Elvin Starr now, sir? When may we expect him back?'

'He's in America. I had a postcard from him a day or two ago. He mentioned that he'd sold a television script and would be able to clear up all his debts.'

'Indeed?' Odd Job was making a list of the property now. 'I suppose you don't happen to have kept the postcard, sir?'

'No, I don't suppose I have.'

'I'll take a look at the other rooms, if you don't mind, sir.' When he returned he said: 'I shall have to make a few inquiries. I'll be back with a colleague in a few days.'

'Wait a moment,' I said. 'It's just possible I put Elvin's card in this drawer. Yes, here it is.' I produced a card with a Miami postmark. 'He says he'll be back on 25 February and I can have use of the flat till then.'

Odd Job read slowly through the postcard, which was addressed to Martin Starr. 'Ah well, that's rather different. I'll call back then. Let's hope your brother will be able to settle this little matter.' He thanked me for my co-operation and departed.

Anticipating this visit, I had made a neat safety play while I was in America. The idea had occurred to me after a similar encounter with one of the Social Security busybodies. 25 February was several weeks ahead, and one way or another I would have raised some cash by then. I have become quite an expert in the art of borrowing. These are some of my cardinal rules:

Don't try to borrow from the rich. If they were in the habit of lending large sums they wouldn't be rich, and if you ask for a small sum they despise you.

Don't borrow from any girl you're interested in. Even if you pay her back it will sour the relationship.

For slightly different reasons, don't borrow within the family. I wouldn't ask my parents for money; still less my tit-nosed elder brother.

Broadly speaking, you can raise cash from three types: the generous-complacent, the greedy and the unwary.

By generous-complacent I mean the people who like the feeling of being able to help someone less fortunate. It's wise to pay back this type fairly soon if you can. You may be able to come again, and meanwhile they may give you some good publicity ('Elvin may borrow, but he always pays you back').

The greedy are the easiest. You don't offer them interest as such but you let them think they are on to a good bet. I have several good ploys in this category.

The unwary are those who, willingly or not, will take a post-dated cheque. When the time comes, it may or may not be convenient to meet the cheque; in my case, usually not.

Of course, I'm not always hard up. My problem lies in what the business wallahs call cash flow. When everything goes well and I turn over perhaps £1,000 in a fortnight, I tend to live up to it, partly because I hate scrimping and partly because people won't pay you £100 for a pro date if you look as though you haven't got the price of a haircut. When I get a bad run I'm short of cash, inevitably. At present, because of the commitment to Habib, I didn't have much time for pro dates, my luck at poker was vile, and I had no capital. So I was doubly pleased to get a call from Helga that seemed to contain a likely proposition with no immediate outlay. After exchanging greetings I asked her what had been happening while I was away.

'Too little for my liking. There has been a lot of talk about the trials for Monte Carlo. I'll tell you about that later, I'm ringing you now about something else: you remember I told you that Frank had it in for Mosey because of that business at the club? Things are beginning to hum and there may be something in it for you. If you're free to come round I'll tell you about it. Frank's out of town.'

I was round at her place within the hour. Her first question when she opened the door was whether the porter had seen me come in. She was wearing fawn-coloured breeches, tucked into leather boots.

Women like to take their time and first we chatted about the current bridge scene. 'They've given up the idea of putting your team in the box,' Helga said, referring to the trials for Monte Carlo. 'They're going to hold a pairs trial in York, to suit the Scottish pairs.'

In York? That was Toni's home town.

'Toni comes from York, doesn't she?' said Helga, reading my thoughts, blast her. 'One day you'll realize that girl's as square as a chessboard. You'll get nowhere, least of all in her home town. Now, do you want to hear about Frank and Mosey?'

'Sure.'

'You know that one of Mosey's sidelines is ramping shares?'

'Doing what to shares?'

'Ramping — you know, boosting. You buy shares in a company, then plug it for all you're worth, pretending you have inside knowledge. If it's not too big a company and you can persuade a few people with money to buy the shares, obviously the price will rise. Mosey has been touting a firm called Monarch Furs. Now it so happens I worked for Monarch at one time. Frank knows the directors and owns a large holding. So when people in the bridge world began to make inquiries, Leonard Fieldsman asked Frank whether there was any strength in the rumours Mosey was putting round. Frank said the business was ticking along normally. At the time he wasn't interested in Mosey's activities. Then this business at the club aroused his Sicilian streak.' Helga took a swig of whisky. 'Do you know anything about options?' she asked me.

'Very little.'

'Then I'll just give you the general picture. Beside buying a large block of shares, Mosey has taken a big Call option, which means he is gambling that the shares will rise. Frank has taken an even bigger Put option, which means he wants the shares to fall. And Frank has a bit of influence, because the chief union official at Monarch is in his pocket. I was friendly with this guy myself at one time.' Helga gave me a bland look. 'There's going to be a strike at the factory before long. Oh God, if I tell you any more I'll end up as a concrete pillar on the M1.'

'I'll look out for you.'

'*Liebling*! This friend of ours, the union official, says the strike can be arranged any time in the next two months. When it happens, Frank will dispose of his shares and there'll be pickets and a great hullabaloo. The shares will drop like a stone and Mosey will be caught with his pants down. Horrible thought,' she added.

Very interesting, this insight into the financial world. It was silly of me, but I didn't see how I could make money out of it.

'By becoming a bear of Monarch Furs, *dummkopf*, and taking a Put option for as much as you can afford. When they go down, you sell at today's price. Don't do it through Leonard, though, go to some broker who doesn't know any of our crowd.'

An excellent feature of this scheme, if it came off, was that I would be able to repay Mosey, in effect, with his own money. He had won a big bet from me during one of the pick-up games at the club. When I gave him a post-dated cheque he squawked like a castrated macaw, but there was nothing he could do about it.

I could place the order for the shares with my stuffed-shirt cousin, Montagu. 'That ne'er-do-well cousin of mine seems to be settling down at last,' he would say to a colleague as he put down the phone.

Helga was sitting with her right leg thrown over her left knee, showing a very attractive length of thigh. 'Business being over,' I said, 'do you remember you promised to show me the rest of the movie strip one day?' There were some photos of Helga in riding gear on the table in the living-room.

'Did I?' She finished her drink slowly. 'All right, this way.' She walked towards the bedroom.

In the last of the photos I had seen, Helga had dismounted from the horse and was standing sideways to the camera, tapping her leg with the riding crop. There were two more on the chest-of-drawers in the bedroom. In the first she was facing the camera, wearing jodphurs only and looking demure; no horse. The second was a back view; just boots and spurs, feet apart, the crop held in both hands across the centre of her buttocks. I shot up like a gun. 'There's one more,' she said, opening a drawer beside the bed.

'Christ!' I exclaimed. 'Does Frank know about this?'

'Don't be silly, he arranged it. Frank's a number one voyeur. Oh, don't get the wrong idea, we have quite a good relationship, up to a point.'

I was boiling over by this time. I bundled Helga on to the bed, making a successful grab at the zip of her breeches. I soon realized she was as keen as I was. I forced her to her knees and a wiggle of her bottom signified her approval. That final photo had given me the idea. The animals can't all be wrong.

When I arrived back at my place after this enjoyable interlude, Gavin was sitting on the stairs. Gavin is a coloured youth, one of the squatters on the top floor. The first time I saw him, about six months ago, he had threatened me with a knife and demanded 'bread'. As he was pissed to the eyebrows, it wasn't difficult to kick the knife out of his hand and knock him out. There was no percentage in making enemies of the brethren upstairs, so I pulled him into the flat and let him sleep it off. We became quite good friends later.

He came in now and I told him the story of our trip to Miami, including the mysterious mugging of Maurice. He asked me to go through the events of the day again, including the encounter with Hank and Larry at the Jai-Alai. Then he said, 'Do you think it's possible it was meant for you?' This hadn't occurred to me. Gavin's a smart boy.

At the club the following day I had a talk with Miles Lang. He asked about Miami and then gave me the latest information about the trials for Monte Carlo.

'They're going to hold a trial for twelve pairs,' he said. 'The first two will qualify by right. We've got to toil up to York. The only good thing about that is that there's racing at Beverley.'

'Is one of your horses running?' I asked. Miles only owned a horse and a half, but I knew the question would please him.

'No, but it's with my trainer. If you're interested, come down to my place in Epsom and watch the final gallop. It'll be in about a fortnight. Meanwhile, keep it under your hat.'

In my present state of health I couldn't miss any chance. If Helga was right, the crisis at Monarch Furs would occur at about the same time as the big race. I might bring off a double.

First I had to speak to Hervey about the trials. 'The selectors have buggered us up as usual,' I said to him one afternoon. 'We won't be able to play as a threesome. What shall we do about Maurice?'

'Edward Clinton and I are playing together in the Masters Pairs, as you know,' Hervey replied. 'He might like to play in the trials as well. Then you could play with Maurice.' Was Hervey being diplomatic? It was difficult to tell.

Toni and some friends joined us in the bar before dinner. After we had endured a description by Arthur Mainwaring of some boring hand he had played in the afternoon, Toni turned the conversation to the European women's pairs, which was due to be played at Monte Carlo in the week before the world championship. Toni's usual partner, Laura Durston, couldn't get away because of some family anniversary, and Julia Lang had asked Toni to play with her.

'Watch it,' I said. 'She's after your ass.'

'I must admit the same idea occurred to me,' said Hervey,

'though I may not have expressed it so elegantly. I have advised Toni against it.'

'What about Penfold?' I asked. 'Has she been relegated?'

'Rhoda's going to play with Jilly Lucas,' said Toni. 'They've been booked to score in the world championship the week after.' Jilly Lucas was Maurice's bird from Manchester.

The final gallop for Miles's horse was due on the following Thursday. We went down by train the previous evening and took a taxi in the direction of Epsom Downs. 'The house is pretty full, with the boys home,' said Miles. 'We'll have to put you up at the lodge.'

As it was quite late, and an early start was threatened, I got out at the lodge. I had been asleep for about ten minutes, or so it seemed, when a quavering retainer shook my shoulder and said, 'Half-past six, sir. Mr Miles is expecting you for breakfast at seven o'clock.'

Miles, wearing a landed gentry suit of green and yellow dogtooth, was practising chip shots on the lawn when I arrived. 'Come along in,' he said, leading the way to the dining-room. 'The *au pair* has to get the children up, so we shall have to fend for ourselves.' There was an array of silver dishes, containing eggs, bacon, sausages, mushrooms, the lot.

As we left the dining-room we heard shrill cries from upstairs, but none of the family appeared. 'It can be quite chilly up on the downs, you'd better take this,' said Miles, throwing me a sheepskin coat which was much too big for me and a pair of outsize binoculars. 'Wait here and I'll fetch the bus.'

The 'bus' turned out to be a vintage Bentley, with a raised driving seat. We proceeded down the drive with a series of cranking noises and posterior explosions.

When we arrived at the stables I was struck by the number of cars. 'Do so many owners come to watch the gallops?' I asked.

Miles laughed at my innocence. 'These belong to the lads,' he said. 'If they need extra cash for a new car at any time, they go on strike.'

We dismounted and stood in a sort of quadrangle. A wizened

ancient, laughingly described as 'head lad', approached us. 'Mr Stephen's on the phone,' he informed us. 'He'll be out soon.'

After several minutes a horsey-looking type with a cloth cap, craggy eyebrows, and brick-red face, emerged from the house. 'This is Stephen Carless,' said Miles with a respectful air. 'Stephen, this is a friend of mine from London.' Red-face gave me a curt nod, evidently agreeing with Miles that my name was not worth mentioning.

We drove a short distance to the downs in Red-face's Range Rover. The sun had begun to appear through the mist and the atmosphere was exhilarating. There were already gallops in progress. I noted that some of the 'lads' were lasses. Not bad either; it was nice to see the way they stretched their breeches when at full gallop.

'Our nag will be running with three others,' Miles explained. 'They start from the stalls over there and will go about $4\frac{1}{2}$ furlongs. It's the jockey with the red sweater and red helmet. The animal's name is Mish Mish.'

'Mish Mish?'

'Yes, the owner is an Arab. It's part of a well-known saying, "*Boukra f'il mish mish*", meaning "tomorrow when the apricot blossoms". For example, someone asks you "When do you expect a reply from the Gas Board?" and that's your philosophical answer. More poetic than "when pigs fly".'

The four horses came out in a line and our selection soon showed in front. Over the last two hundred yards, however, the others closed on him and Mish Mish finished a moderate third. I prepared a few words of condolence, but Miles and the trainer did not seem in the least put out. Red-face went to speak to the jockey and Miles said:

'If that means what I think it means, it was bloody fantastic.'

Red-face returned and said, 'Safe to speak in front of him?' Miles nodded and Red-face went on: 'The first two were three-year-olds who ought to be able to give our fellow 17 lbs at this time of year. The one that finished last is a two-year-old which has already won a race.'

'Reg was wearing his belt?' asked Miles a little anxiously.

'Oh, sure. 21 lbs of lead round his middle.'

This, presumably, was to deceive any kibitzers who might be lurking in the bushes. The affair had all the elements of a con trick, so far as I was concerned, but Miles seemed quite happy about it. He had a few words alone with Red-face before we left.

Declining a not-very-pressing invitation to stay for lunch, I picked up my things at the lodge and Miles drove me to the station.

'The tricky part of this operation,' he said, 'will be to get the money on at a good price. Mish Mish has run once, showing little form, so the first price ought to be about 8 to 1. I have promised to put £1,000 on for Stephen at the first show. If we tried to do this on the course it would ruin the price. The owner doesn't bet, which solves one problem, but I want £3,000 for myself at the starting price. We've got to place the early money in the betting shops. They'll normally let you have at least a part of your bet at first show, the rest at S P. It's essential to spread the money round in small amounts, otherwise it will get back to the course and the price will tumble. Bookies are very careful in two-year-old races, because horses can improve very quickly. Unfortunately, the race comes in the middle of the trials, so neither of us can be in London to organize.'

'I might be able to find some layabouts to do the leg-work,' I said, thinking of Gavin and his friends. 'There are some squatters in the place where I live. Most of them would be happy to earn a tenner.'

'Can they be trusted with the cash, though? Suppose we had a team of six, they'd be carrying about £500 each. With a bit of effort I could place the remaining £1,000 on the telephone without affecting the price.'

'Ah well, that's another matter. Could it be done in short bursts? For example, the boys could go out with £100 each to place in the morning. Then they could go back to headquarters for another £100, and so on. They'd have the betting slips as evidence.'

'Possibly, but we'd have to examine the time factor. The problem is going to be the £1,000 on the first show. The big multiple firms have a very good intelligence service. Any move for an outsider in a two-year-old race would very quickly be picked up. Mosey, at the club, might be able to help with this. He mentioned to me some time ago that a friend of his had a chain of shops in the area. This chap might be able to distribute the money without anyone catching on.'

Mosey again? I wouldn't trust him more than a couple of inches. There seemed to be so many holes in this operation.

'Can you really hope to stop the news getting round?' I asked Miles. 'For example, Reg, with his loaded chastity belt, must know what's going on.'

'Reg won't be riding in the race. Anyway, he wouldn't give you a cold.'

Unforthcoming Reg might be, but would that stop him trying to make a few hundred for himself? My train was in the station now, and I told Miles I'd have a word with Gavin about getting the money on.

Gavin reported that several of his friends invested a large part of their (social security) income in the betting shops. This was good, because the manager of a betting shop is less likely to pay attention to bets from a 'face' than from a new customer. What's more, the boys would know the betting shop routine. Gavin didn't think we need worry about any of the boys running off with the cash. 'Even with £500 they'd be too lazy to fuck off and start a new life,' he said. 'We can keep their cards and personal belongings as insurance. If necessary, we can sit on the heads of their girlfriends as well.'

Before we left for York, every detail of the operation was planned and rehearsed. The boys would place as much as they could early on at their usual betting haunts, then a car would drop them one at a time in the area covered by Mosey's pal, ready to leap in at the first show, then rush to another shop in the neighbourhood. Apart from his own bet, Miles was laying out plenty: £1,000 for Red-face, £100 to Mosey's pal for laying off the bets discreetly, £50 to Gavin, £20 for each of the boys. The animal had better win. I intended to risk £100 each way on my own account. I asked Helga if she would like me to put anything on for her. She laughed and said she had backed one of Miles's good things a year ago.

On the first morning in York Toni's father gave a cocktail party. Toni was there, of course, and old Laura Durston. Maurice renewed acquaintance with the ancient aunt whose speciality was cathedral architecture. Most of the talk was about the trials. The selectors were pledged to consult the first two pairs about the choice of third pair, and everyone was assuring everyone else of unqualified support should this situation arise.

Hervey and Edward made a good start but we set them back in the third round when Edward forgot about the strong pass in our system, misplaced the cards, and lost a disastrous 800. This shook the old gentleman badly and we won the match 20–0.

The next morning was the day of the big race. Mish Mish was due to run in the two o'clock at Beverley. Miles spent an hour on the telephone, placing £1,000 in small amounts. I borrowed a street map from the hall porter, who showed me where the betting shops were located. Scraping the bottom of the barrel, I had managed to get hold of £200 in cash. I traipsed around for two hours, distributing £100 each way for myself and £200 on the nose for Miles.

It was already a quarter to two when I got back to the hotel. The afternoon session was due to start at 2.15, so we were pressed for time. We had arranged to watch the race in Miles's room. As I crossed to the lift I was buttonholed by Maurice.

'Where have you been, I've been looking for you all the morning,' he said irritably. 'We have to talk about the two diamond sequences before the next session. You remember we didn't decide whether after the second relay the opener should show his fragment or his splinter.'

'I have to take a call in my room,' I said, thinking quickly. 'Personal call, from Geneva. I'll be down as soon as I can.' Habib was in Geneva at the moment.

Miles was fuming when he let me into his room. 'The racing hasn't even started yet,' he said. 'The news went on interminably, all about some bloody yachtsman arriving at

Southampton in his sodding boat. Now it's the damned advertisements.' A freckled kiddie was extolling the delights of Brekky Brik. 'If I could get my hands on that brat, I'd wring its ruddy neck...'

'Dear little chap,' I said.

Miles's impatience was exaggerated, because when eventually the picture dissolved into a racing scene the runners were still in the paddock. 'No. 11, Mish Mish,' said the commentator. 'A bay colt by So Blessed out of a Petingo mare. He's had one race, at Warwick, and has evidently come on since then. No. 5 is Red Duster, by Red God, out of an Abwah mare, so he's bred for speed. On his good second to Hi Lo at Lingfield last month he's the likely favourite, but let's see how they figure in the market.'

Now the first show went up on the screen: 9/4 Red Duster, 5/2 Mish Mish, 6 Basra, 8 bar.

Mish Mish had been among the 10/1 others in the morning papers.

Miles went white with rage. 'You get a chance for a coup like this about once a year,' he said, 'and then some bastard buggers it up. One of your boys must have talked.'

'I don't think so,' I said. 'They weren't told the name of the horse until just before they went into the shop.'

The price on Mish Mish shortened with every show. As they went into the stalls it was 6/4 Mish Mish, 11/4 Red Duster, 8 Basra, 10 bar three.

'They're under starter's orders,' announced the commentator. 'They're off! Valkyrie is first to show, from Dresden and Red Duster ... Mish Mish was slowly into his stride, is next to last ... Red Duster has taken it up, with Mish Mish improving ... At the two furlong mark it's Red Duster from Mish Mish, these two well clear of Basra and Dresden ... Mish Mish, on the stand side, is gaining on Red Duster ... 50 yards to go, there's nothing in it ... Mish Mish slightly ahead, but Red Duster's coming again ... At the post it looks like Red Duster from here, but we'll have to wait for the photo.'

It was obvious from the picture of the re-run that Red Duster had got up at the finish. A minute later the result was announced: 'First, No. 5, Red Duster; second, No. 11, Mish Mish; third, No. 2, Dinah . . .'

'I know someone who was at the course,' said Miles stonily. 'I'll ring him this evening and find out what happened to the price. We have to go down now.'

Miles seemed to be more concerned about the blow to his self-esteem than the loss of his money. For me it was a disaster. The return on my place bet would cover only about one third of my win bet. I wouldn't have enough cash left for my hotel bill and it would be stupid to give them a dud cheque.

There was another hammer blow while I was changing for dinner. Helga was on the phone from London:

'Listen, my love, I've some bad news for you,' she began. 'I tried to get hold of you this morning before the market closed, but they couldn't find you. You went into that Monarch business, didn't you? Well, there's been a take-over bid, the strike is off, and Frank has gone into reverse. You'd better close your bear, there's nothing to be done about the options, they're a write-off.'

I only half understood the financial gobbledygook, but obviously cousin Montagu's firm was going to be added to the list of my creditors. My situation now was desperate. The first instalment of Habib's retainer had come and gone. After I had settled the judgment summons, paid the rent, and temporarily averted the persistence of the Inland Revenue, I hadn't a penny in my bank accounts and I still owed Mosey, among others. After the evening session I tackled Maurice.

'When are we due for the next instalment from Shoukry?'

'In about eight weeks.'

'Do you think I could ask him for an advance?'

'No.'

'Well, can you advance me, say, £1,000 until we collect?'

'No.'

'For God's sake, Maurice, why not? I'm in a bit of hole at the moment.'

'Firstly, I can't afford it. I have to live, too. Secondly, how do I know you'd be able to repay me? I could let you have £200 at most. You'd have to write a letter to Habib authorizing him to pay that amount to me when the next instalment was due.'

'Bit infra dig, that.'

'Then ask him to pay the whole amount into a specific bank account. You and I could have a double signature agreement so that you'd have to pay me back before you could take anything out yourself.'

Bloody little Shylock! I had to agree.

Later in the evening Miles reported on his conversation with the friend who had been at Beverley. One or two of the outside bookies had put up 5/1 Mish Mish and there had been a tiny knockover. It was immediately scrubbed, and when the market opened in the big ring the price was 5/2.

'It wasn't one of the professionals,' said Miles, still brooding over who had spilled the beans. 'I'm sure of that. They wouldn't dare to doublecross me. It wouldn't have been the manager of the betting shop, either. You say it couldn't have been one of your boys. That leaves Mosey.'

'I thought so all along. Still, it's some consolation that he must have lost his money, too.'

'Doesn't follow, I'm afraid. It could have been cronies of his who took the early 5/1. They could have laid it back at 2/1 later.'

Funny that an insignificant little twerp like Mosey should be at the centre of these two operations. He had come out of the Monarch affair smelling of rosewater, and for all we knew he had made a profit from the racing coup as well. Meanwhile, I had lost my money both ways.

As if I hadn't enough worries, Helga had been right about Toni: on her home ground she just wouldn't play. The following afternoon I caught her on her own and tried to manoeuvre her to my room.

'Don't be silly,' she said. 'If I so much as set foot in the lift there'll be talk.'

'Why the hell do you have to bother with these wall-eyed old gossips?'

'Keep your voice down. I live in this town, remember.' She walked off, leaving me in a furious temper.

A minute or two later I was collecting my key from the porter's desk when the swing doors revolved and a slight figure entered, attired in motor-cycling gear and carrying a small case. She removed her helmet, scattering raindrops over the mat. When she took off her goggles I saw it was Rhoda Penfold.

'The TT race is next week,' I called across.

'Hullo there! I've ridden fifty miles in the rain to watch you play tonight. Just to see if I'm missing anything.'

'That's great. Shall we have a drink in the bar before dinner?'

'Right. Just give me a few minutes to get out of this clobber.'

When she emerged from the cloakroom ten minutes later her short hair was crisp and tidy, her cheeks flushed from the ride. Instead of her usual scruffy jeans she was wearing a turquoise skirt and a white blouse. 'My!' I exclaimed. 'Now I see what they mean by Hell's Angels.'

We found a quiet corner in the bar. She wanted to know how the trials were progressing. I told her that one of the Scottish pairs looked like winning and that Maurice and I would be lucky to finish second.

'You looked in a terrible temper when I first saw you in the hall,' she remarked. 'What had got into you?'

I didn't think it would be tactful to tell her that I was upset because I wasn't getting anywhere with the girl I really wanted. Transposing the date and adding a few colourful touches, I recounted the story of the racing coup that had proved so unlucky. 'Naturally I was wild,' I ended.

She looked at me over her glass. 'I adore men who are wild,' she said.

This seemed to tie up with Toni's account of Rhoda's activities with Julia. Anyway, it was a pretty fair invitation and I took it up at once. 'We don't have to go into dinner for forty minutes or so,' I said. 'I'm going up to my room now. When you've finished your drink, take the lift to the second floor. Room 218, I'll leave the door slightly open.' I nodded to the barman and walked out, giving her no chance to answer.

Had I played it the right way, I wondered, when I reached my room. She might be less keen than I thought or she might lose her nerve. Funny, I hadn't thought much about her in the past, but tonight she seemed more feminine and very desirable.

I should have realized she wasn't the type to be shy of stepping into the lift in a strange hotel. I had just had a quick wash and put on a clean shirt when she slipped in. She came straight into my arms. Her shoulders beneath the silk blouse were thin and bony, like a boy's, her breasts small but neat. I held her close and moved my hand up and down her back.

'I'm going to beat this adorable bottom before you leave,' I whispered in her ear.

'Promises, promises!'

'Oh, I mean it. We haven't got a lot of time, so prepare for chastisement.'

Without a word she unzipped her skirt and let it fall to the floor. As she stepped out and turned round to lay it on a chair, I glimpsed two little pink cheeks, half hidden by the blouse and miniscule French pants. I walked to the dressing-table and picked up a hairbrush.

'Hell, you're not going to use that,' she said. 'I thought you were just going to spank me.'

'Certainly I'm going to use it.' My role was to be masterful. 'Bend over the bed.' I tested the brush against the palm of my hand. It had a good grip and a flat back about four inches long, covered in leather.

'Warm me up first with your hand,' she pleaded.

I saw no objection to this. I sat on the bed and she stood in front of me, still in her shoes and stockings.

'Do you want me to take off my blouse and pants?' she asked.

'You can keep the blouse on. I'll deal with the rest.' I pulled her pants down slowly. 'Now lie flat across my lap.'

She lay lengthwise, the bottom of the blouse coyly covering the target area. I folded it to the small of her back and surveyed her taut behind. There were shadowy marks on both cheeks, evidently Julia's handiwork. Rhoda must have known this but she made no comment. I moved my left hand under her breast.

I began with a dozen smart spanks on each side, bringing warm blood to the surface. She wiggled her bottom from side to side, but otherwise there was no response. I continued to spank her, covering both cheeks. 'Mmm,' she said when I paused, 'that was nice. Let's go on like this, you don't need the hairbrush.'

'Oh yes we do,' I said. I lifted her off my lap and picked up the brush. 'Now bend over.'

She gave me a reproachful look and inclined hesitantly over the side of the bed.

'Tighter than that.'

She bent her knees and lowered her head until it touched the bedclothes. I lifted the blouse and made a business of adjusting her till her buttocks were curved at precisely the right angle.

'I'm going to start with four strokes on this side,' I told her, marking the spot with the cool, hard back, 'then four on this side.'

The preliminary spanking must have lessened the sting, because she accepted these first eight strokes without a murmur, though her buttocks tensed each time the brush landed. For the next two or three minutes I whacked her vigorously, watching the twin cheeks change colour from pink to rosy, from rosy to crimson, from crimson to blue, then to purple with a whitish rim. I extended the range slightly, applying the brush to areas that had not so far felt the full force of the leather. After two or three of these she jumped up and tried to reach for her clothes, crying 'That's enough, Elvin! I can't take any more.'

'I'll tell you when you've had enough,' I said. Sitting on the bed, I pulled her between my knees and forced her head to the floor. Gripping tightly and holding her in position with my left hand, I gave her a final dozen. She was whimpering at every stroke now and struggling to get free.

When I released her she rose stiffly to her feet and glared at me, tears in her eyes, massaging her bruised behind with both hands. Then she moved to a wall mirror, turned on the light, and looked over her shoulder to study the marks. 'Just look what you've done, you brute,' she said. 'I won't be able to sit down for a week. I'll have to ride home with my bum in the air, like Lester Piggott.'

The reflection in the mirror resembled two big, round

damsons. We kissed passionately. 'Now fuck me,' she said suddenly.

We lay side by side for a while, then I turned on my back and we adopted the Roman position. As I thrust upwards she leaned forward and I grasped the warm hardness of her buttocks. The way she had been wriggling, I didn't think she could have any strength left. I was wrong, we came together in a mighty spasm.

The others had started dinner when we came down and we settled at a table for two, ignoring inquisitive glances. While we were consuming what passed for *boeuf Stroganoff*, I asked Rhoda what was the state of play between her and Julia.

'There's been a slight coolness. It'll pass off.'

I naturally wanted to know what Julia would say when confronted with the posterior evidence of Rhoda's unfaithfulness. 'Will Julia be annoyed if she hears that you and I have been seen together?' I asked, approaching the subject warily.

'No, why should she be?'

'Well, you know what I mean,' I said, stumbling on. 'Is there any danger that she'll find out about our little scene?'

'You mean, what will Julia say if she sees my backside looking like a tropical sunset? I'll have a raspberry ice, please.'

'Just coffee for me. That's what I had in mind, yes.'

'She'll be thrilled.'

'She won't be jealous? I thought there was some trouble in Madrid when you were going round with that Spanish chap.'

'Lopez, you mean? No, Julia's funny. She doesn't mind me having sex with men so long as she can contribute in her own way.'

'What does she want. A threesome?'

'Of a kind. You might enjoy it. Lopez wouldn't play at first, but on the last night in Madrid we had a whale of a time. Look, they're calling you. You'll have to go. Keep me a chair beside your table. A soft one.'

Maurice and I were in good form and had established a useful lead by half time. Toni came in later and she and Rhoda sat giggling in a corner. Rhoda left before the end of the session. We won this match, and both matches on the last day, so in the end we finished second to the Scottish pair, Orton and MacBride. Orton lives in London and is a useful player. Hervey and Clinton were third, Miles and Leonard sixth.

By the terms of the contest the selectors had to consult the first two pairs about the choice of third pair. The Scots made a routine bid in favour of their countrymen, who had finished fifth. When I was asked, I suggested that Hervey, Maurice and I should form a threesome. This was safe, because I knew the selectors would not depart from the formula they had announced. Maurice, who didn't have to worry about Hervey, voted for Miles and Leonard. 'They won't be nervous of anyone and they have a touch of class.'

The selectors announced the team soon afterwards: the first two pairs in the trials, plus Miles and Leonard. Hervey and Edward put a good ass on it, warmly congratulating all three pairs.

I didn't feel well the next morning and took a later train than the others, so I had time for reflection. Perhaps it was my jaundiced eye, but it seemed to me that the bridge world was buzzing with hostility. Take Mosey, for instance: Frank Rowlands was out for his blood because of the incident at the club, and Miles because of the racing affair. Mosey himself would burst a blood vessel if he knew what Frank had tried to do to him over the shares. Then I thought about Habib, always so smooth on the surface. He must have noticed Maurice's obscene ogling of Rosanna. Was it possible that he organized the attack on Maurice as a warning? The atmosphere in Miami had been strange in many ways. I wasn't at all sure that the poker game had been straight. It might have penetrated to Brindley that he had been conned on the tennis court and he might have arranged a crooked poker game to get his money back. Just one stacked deal would be enough. And there was a mystery surrounding Ross: what was he up to, associating with that riff-raff on the boat?

There were tensions on the domestic front, too. Sooner or later Frank would catch up with Helga. I had the feeling that

Hervey and Toni were disenchanted with one another. And there was something distinctly odd about Miles's relations with his family.

Thinking of Ross again, it occurred to me that I hadn't entered in my little black book the money I owed him from the poker game. The more I looked at the list of my debts, the more alarming they seemed. Electricity and telephone bills had reached the 'red' stage, I would have to do something about those. I had paid the rent, but rates were six months in arrears. The tax buggers were off my back for the moment, but they'd be at me again before long. Heaven knows how much I owed cousin Montagu's firm; anyway, they'd have to wait. Of my personal creditors, Mosey was not the largest but he was the most pressing. It was his amiable practice, whenever I left the club, to call loudly, 'Mind how you cross the road.' This was bad for my reputation. In the same way it was time I paid something back to Hervey, as I had owed him various amounts for over a year.

The next contribution from Habib wouldn't see me straight by any means. My best hope for raising some immediate cash was the Cavendish Club Pairs. This event carried enormous prize and sweep money and I had made a tentative arrangement to play with one of the top Americans. (Maurice, I knew, would be appalled by the $1,000 entry fee.) My plan was to approach perhaps three different people, each in the strictest confidence, with a simple proposition: 'Advance the money for my entry fee and air ticket and you can have 25 per cent of my action.' Arthur Mainwaring was a likely prospect, it would flatter him to be asked. If I found two or three backers and did well in the event I would have to pay out a large slice of my winnings, but in the meanwhile I would have much needed cash in hand.

Back in London, I told Gavin what had happened up north. He already knew, of course, that Mish Mish had lost at a short price, but he didn't agree that Mosey was responsible for the leak. 'Miles is only guessing, isn't he? My money would be on the jockey or trainer.' If that was right, and Miles ever found out, it would have a shattering effect on his ego. 'And I'll tell you something else,' Gavin added. 'I bet you Hervey's as sick as hell about being left out of the team for the world championship.'

Yes, he probably was. It's funny, I suppose the man in the street thinks that tournament bridge is a civilized pastime for intellectuals, whereas in fact it's more like a pool full of hungry piranhas.

I felt like death the next day and had to stay in bed. A virus, my quack said, concealing his ignorance in the manner of his tribe. Helga brought me grapes and solace of a different kind. Gavin did the shopping. When I felt reasonably human again I rang Toni on an evening when I knew Hervey would be at the club.

'Hi, beautiful. What's new?'

'Nothing special. Oh, I was speaking to Miles just before you rang. You know the rest of your team has been playing practice matches against teams from the midlands? They lost two out of three. Miles says the Picts were diabolical.'

I hadn't heard. It didn't surprise me.

'Is Hervey crusty about not being in the team?' I asked.

'I don't think so. He quite fancies the idea of being match manager. Edward is disappointed, though.'

'Edward? He gave me a long spiel to the effect that he was just making up the numbers in the trial and didn't reckon on playing in Monte Carlo even if he happened to qualify.'

'Be your age.'

I turned to more personal matters. 'You promised to have dinner with me, remember?'

'But you're a sick man.'

'So I need a tonic.'

'This week's not easy. My only free day is tomorrow.'

'Tomorrow's fine. I'm still feeling a bit frail but I have my appetite back.'

'I bet.'

'Yes, well, I'll have to be a little ungallant and ask you to come here. I'm supposed to be landlocked, but I could totter down to the Chinky restaurant in the next block. Will that suit you?'

'Provided we don't travel by taxi.'

Ignoring this unsubtle reference to the episode in Madrid, I said I would expect her about 7.30.

The next day seemed interminable. I rang Miles, to hear the full story of the matches they had played in Nottingham. I even tried to study Maurice's thesis on the sequences following the two diamond opening in Habib's system. Eventually 7.30 arrived, and 7.45 and 8.00. I was beginning to panic when at ten past eight the buzzer sounded. Toni was wearing a brown skirt and a cream blouse with an amber necklace. 'How adorable you look,' I said, 'and what perfect timing!'

During the meal we talked about the trials, the prospects for Monte Carlo, Toni's new partnership with Julia. I kept off personal topics. The test would come later.

'The coffee's awful here,' I said after the toffee apple. 'Shall we have some coffee and brandy at my place?' This passed off all right. Back at the flat I put the coffee on and brought out the brandy glasses.

'I'll pour my own, thanks.'

'That wouldn't wet the whistle of a canary.' I added a reasonable amount.

'You're not going to get me tight, Elvin.' She raised the glass to her lips and gave me a mischievous smile.

At this moment there were sounds of a commotion in the street. I went to the window overlooking the Bayswater Road. A posse of men seemed to be battering on the front door. I heard the sound of someone running down from above, there was a knock on my door and an urgent cry of 'Elvin! Are you there? Let me in for Christ's sake.' It was Gavin, looking scared.

'It's the sheriffs.' He meant, a combined force of police and bailiffs. 'They're going to create hell.' Toni had stepped backwards when the fracas began, and now he saw her for the first time. 'Gee, ma'am, pardon the intrusion,' he said, in a fair imitation of Gary Cooper at his most courtly.

Large feet were pounding up the stairs and there were bangings on the floor above. It hardly seemed the moment for formal introductions: Miss Cory, may I present Mr Nogumbopo?'

'Pour yourself a brandy and sit down,' I said to Gavin. 'We were just going to have some coffee.'

'Well, thanks, if I could stay for a few minutes. If the sheriffs find any hash they pull everyone in and keep them at the Bastille till four in the morning. As soon as they leave, I can push off.'

Toni seemed to be completely unnerved. 'I must go now,' she said, gulping down her coffee. Gavin offered to leave, but I could see it would make no difference whether he went or stayed. The spell was broken.

I watched the lights of her taxi disappear and exchanged a word with the rearguard of the sheriffs. As I climbed the stairs I wondered, When am I going to make it with that girl? Is that blooming apricot ever going to blossom?

Monte Carlo

by Toni Cory

There is a knock on the door and I give Hervey a nudge. He sits up, blinking, and calls '*Entrez!*' Hervey's French, *très Anglais*, goes well with his striped pyjamas. We're staying at the Metropole, one of the gracious, old-fashioned hotels in Monte Carlo.

The waiter comes in with our *petit déjeuner* – brioches, croissants and all the trimmings. How cleverly he balances the double tray! As the dressing-table is cluttered with my things and the bedside-table is too small, he places it neatly on the luggage-rack.

'*Le Figaro pour Monsieur?*'

'*Merci,*' ventures Hervey, rashly. His ideas of French were picked up on business trips to Belgium. Let's hope the waiter won't try to keep this conversation going.

I pour the coffee, using the strainer for the hot milk. Hervey looks up anxiously. 'Don't worry, I'm using the *passoir.*' (Must be careful about that word.) Hervey goes into a tantrum if there are any 'floating bits', as he calls them.

'Don't get jam on the bedclothes,' he says automatically. It is a well known fact that French knives are always looking for a chance to slide off the tray. Just once a jammy knife fell on the bedclothes, and Hervey never lets me forget it.

Now he is completely immersed in his paper. I don't understand why men make such a fuss about the newspapers when they're abroad. You'd think they'd be glad to forget for a few days about strikes, inflation, cold wars, and the rest of it. In

Biarritz last summer Miles complained every day because the Herald Tribune carried news of the Baltimore Bounders, or whatever, and didn't give the cricket scores.

Whoops! There goes the knife again. Luckily I catch it just in time and Hervey doesn't notice. Evidently he can understand the advertisements in the *Figaro*, for his next remark is:

'Sadlers Wells are doing Tristan at the *Opéra*. Shall we go?'

'That would be splendid *if* I liked Wagner, which you know I don't, and *if* I weren't playing in the Pairs.'

'So you are. Tell me, how are things going with Julia?'

He means sex-wise, the dirty bastard, but if I answer that way he'll pretend he meant bridge-wise. So I say:

'Not bad for a new partnership. We're lying about sixth. Better than any of the other British girls, anyway.'

Now he *has* to ask:

'Any, er, ambiguous advances so far?'

'She offered to oil my back at the pool yesterday.'

'Oho, many a romance has started that way. It's not far from your back to . . .'

'Shut up, Hervey, you're worse than Elvin.'

'That reminds me, when are you going to tell me the story of your dinner date with Elvin?'

'Nothing to it. We had dinner at a Chinese restaurant and went back to his pad for coffee and brandy. Then there was this hullabaloo I told you about, police and bailiffs. One of the squatters from the top floor came banging at the door, a rather dishy black boy, wearing skin-tight crimson jeans. Elvin and this boy were on Christian-name terms, there was something odd about the relationship. I felt uncomfortable and left soon afterwards.'

'Probably his catamite.'

Catamite? I vaguely associated the word with the Emperor Tiberius in retirement at Capri. I wasn't going to let on to Hervey that I didn't know what it meant, but I looked it up later. 'Sodomite's minion.' Elvin ambidextrous? I wonder. Could be.

On the way to the bathroom I caught a glimpse of my hair in

the mirror. 'God, my hair looks awful,' I said. 'I must get it done before the afternoon.'

'Nonsense, it's perfect.' He hadn't taken his eyes off his newspaper. 'You had it done yesterday, or the day before.'

'*Three* days ago, to be precise. The climate here is disastrous for hair.'

'Why don't you adopt a simple no-nonsense style like Julia's?'

Isn't that just like a man! Julia's hair is always beautifully done, she must go to the hairdresser every day.

'What a good idea!' I said. 'Willingly! Just you buy me the Hermes and Gucci outfits to go with it, that's all.'

I began thinking about my partnership with Julia. I liked playing with her, but could there really be any future in it for a plain Sagittarius like me?

'Hervey!' I yelled from the bath. 'Do you realize that Julia is Scorpio with Capricorn rising?'

'Good heavens! You don't say!' A pause. 'Is that good or bad?'

'It doesn't go with Sagittarius, that's all.'

Laura Durston, my usual partner, is Capricorn, but on the cusp with Sagittarius. We never have a cross word. Laura couldn't come for the Pairs because of some anniversary or other, but she's going to score in the Bermuda Bowl, which starts tomorrow.

'Are you going to Nice to meet the boys?' I asked, as I struggled into my primrose pleated skirt. Hell, don't say I need a 12 now.

'No, I have some business to attend to.'

Hervey and his 'little chats with a colleague in the business'! Some of his friends are very odd people indeed. It seems there's a lot of skullduggery in the stamp world. He told me once that a Belgian friend who was a dealer in rare stamps had a sideline in stolen documents and forged passports.

After a session at the hairdresser's I joined Rhoda Penfold at a table beside the swimming-pool. 'How are things?' I asked her.

'Moderate. I shan't be sorry when the Bermuda Bowl starts.'

'What's your hotel like?'

'Grotty, compared to this place.'

'I'm not so fond of Monte as of Juan or Deauville, are you?'

'I've never been to Juan or Deauville. Jilly and I are working girls, you know.'

Oh dear, she thinks I'm patronizing her. I tried a new tack:

'Did you know that Peter Rosswick was in the American team? Apparently he and his partner took somebody else's place in the trials and won. It'll be nice to see Ross again.'

'Yes, I heard that. He's a pleasant enough boy, but like you I prefer Elvin. He has a certain style, don't you think?'

Before I could make any comment on this, Rhoda went on:

'And how are things going between you and Julia? Has she made any overtures yet?'

'No, of course not.'

'She will. I always knew she fancied you. I'll give you a tip. If she gets on the subject of men's selfishness, tighten your girdle.'

It was time to get ready for the afternoon session, so this bitchy conversation had to end. Rhoda and Jilly Lucas were nearly bottom in the pairs, which may have accounted for her bad mood. Julia and I had a good final session, finishing fourth.

In the evening there was a champagne buffet at the Sporting Club. They do these things in style. The British table, dotted with little Union Jacks, was one of the largest. Laura told me she was staying with Virginia Trupp, who has a flat here. Funny old Virginia has been coming to Monte Carlo for fifteen years and is a well known character in the town.

At the prize-giving for the women's pairs Julia and I won shagreen cigarette cases. It's funny how people love to win prizes. Julia, who could go into Asprey's any day and buy whatever she wanted, was as pleased as punch.

While the draw was being made for the first round of the Bermuda Bowl I heard a friendly voice behind me saying: 'Rhett, I want to you to meet the Scarlett O'Hara of the bridge world. Rhett Brindley – Toni Cory.' Ross's American partner, large and sandy-haired, was sporting a Hibernian jacket of the sort worn by fancy band-leaders. He looked me up and down, commented 'Nice babe,' and returned to the draw. Ross and I talked for a while. I thought he looked rather thin and peaky for someone coming from Florida.

Britain made a poor start in the championship, drawing 10–10 with Italy, losing 7–13 to India, then going down 1–19 to America. Elvin was in a vile temper after this match and had a row with Maurice, though I don't know what about.

Shoukry Habib, who sponsors Maurice and Elvin, arrived to find that Britain was lying seventh out of eight in the qualifying round. As there was no play in the evening he invited us all to a big party at *La Forêt*. The restaurant is perched on the Corniche above Monte Carlo itself, and sitting outside on the warm, summer evening was divine. Unfortunately Elvin spoilt the occasion by being rude to Maurice. 'Long John has an infallible system for roulette,' he remarked loudly. Maurice had come back from America wearing an eye-patch and Elvin had christened him Long John (Silver), which wasn't kind, because Maurice is knee-high to a grasshopper and sensitive about it. On top of that, Elvin gave the words 'Long John' a suggestive meaning. It amused him to pretend that Maurice had a grand passion for Rosanna – Habib's dark-eyed doll. Our host was certainly not amused. Personally I wouldn't care to get on the wrong side of that one, smooth as he is on the surface. You don't climb from the back streets of Cairo to being a multi-millionaire without a streak of ruthlessness.

Driving down to the casino in a crowded car, Julia put her arm round my shoulder and pressed continuously against my thigh. 'Roulette's too slow, I'm going to play *trente-et-quarante*,' she announced when we got out. 'And a spot of *trente-et-trente-neuf* before the evening's over,' murmured Elvin, who had been in the back of the car.

Knowing that we'd wind up at the casino, I had made up some charts earlier in the day. Elvin was Aries, and as Saturn was entering his Sun he had no chance. I thought of warning him, but he would only say it was superstitious twaddle.

Maurice was coy about his system. 'It's true,' he said, 'I do have a system for roulette. You'll see.' Elvin took a seat at the same table and, as he put it, waited for the oracle to speak. But Maurice was in no hurry. For almost half an hour he just sat there, watching the others. Finally he began to edge in a chip here, a chip there. I couldn't detect any pattern in his play. Elvin had already frittered away most of his chips and now, from perversity, he went the opposite way to Maurice — when he had time, that is, because Maurice made most of his bets at the last moment. Maurice won most of the time, Elvin lost. Suddenly Maurice stopped, collected his chips, and gave up his seat.

'Have you read that new book *Win and Run* by L. E. Vine?' Elvin inquired of the table at large. 'That was dead cunning, Maurice, the way you backed the *dernière douzaine*. Is your system copyright?'

Maurice was not to be drawn. 'It's all in the mind,' he answered. 'You wouldn't understand.'

Before the evening was over, Maurice's girlfriend, Jilly Lucas, appeased my curiosity:

'Maurice believes in the contrariness of fate,' she said. 'More than anything he would like to be tall and handsome, instead of which he's small and ugly (though not, for your ears only, by any means bad in bed). His system is to wait till he sees someone losing who obviously can't afford it. Tonight it was that Italian piece in the green dress, with the false eye-lashes. Wherever she plonked her chips, Maurice did the opposite. When she had a couple of wins he stopped playing.'

Elvin insisted on my joining him for a drink at the bar. He was naturally depressed at the way things were going. I thought the Scottish pair would get the blame, but no! 'Haggis and Porridge have played well,' he told me gloomily. 'We haven't been great, and Miles and Leonard were a disaster against India — at least, Miles was. The American match we couldn't help.'

I slipped away soon after. As I was crossing the square between the casino and the Metropole, it started to rain. Always on the day when I've had my hair done, it's a conspiracy! I ducked under the awning outside a café and a moment later a voice called, 'Hullo, Toni, join me for a drink.' I peered into the shadows; it was Miles, sitting alone with a large brandy in front of him. I felt more like a coffee than another drink, but to humour him I ordered a Dubonnet. 'Any luck?' I asked.

'I played a little blackjack, no good. That woggy fellow who took us to dinner was cleaning up.' He looked at me solemnly. 'I suppose I'm getting the blame for the Indian match especially?'

'I've not heard anything like that,' I said, crossing my fingers below the table.

'A likely story, with Elvin in the team. Fact is, Toni, everything's gone sour for me lately.' He gazed into the depths of his *ballon*, then said unexpectedly: 'I could kill that little runt, Mosey.'

He told me about an attempted racing coup in which Mosey had been involved, and a Stock Exchange venture that had gone wrong.

'Frank bloody Rowlands pulled the plug on the whole operation and left me holding the baby,' he said, without a smile at the mixture of metaphors. 'On top of all that,' he went on, 'Natalie has been more bloody than usual lately.' Natalie is Miles's wife, a shadowy figure in the bridge world. 'If she saw me here with you she'd scratch your eyes out — and mine too.'

'If she's jealous, at least it means she cares.'

Miles looked up and nodded. 'You're thinking of Hervey?'

'Yes, I am. I hardly know whether he has any feelings or not. He never shows any.'

'Hervey has the old-fashioned idea that it's unmanly to show emotion. We were all taught that at school. Most of us grow out of it.'

Miles had been quick to take my point. He's an attractive man, all the women say so. I wonder ... Anyway, I was glad I could tell him truthfully that his luck was due to change very shortly. Jupiter was moving into his sun-sign.

Everyone was behaving strangely this week. Two days later Ross and Rhett invited me to join them for dinner at Loews Hotel. Rhett and I were seated on a banquette and Ross was facing us. Half-way through the meal he suddenly pushed back his chair and held his head in his hands. 'Is something wrong?' I asked.

'Would you mind frightfully if I pushed off?' Ross replied. 'I'm not feeling too well.'

'Are you all right?' Rhett asked. 'Would you like me to go with you?'

'No, please,' said Ross. 'I just want to lie down.' He rose unsteadily to his feet and walked slowly out of the restaurant.

'That was very sudden,' I said to Rhett. 'He hadn't been drinking, to speak of. Has he eaten any shellfish in the last two days?'

Rhett hesitated for a moment, then said, 'It's not that. Pete is subject to migraine, you know. He may have felt one coming on.'

We talked for a while about music and other things. Brindley is one of those outgoing Americans who know how to make a girl feel interesting and pleased with herself. Probably Leo, possibly Gemini, I thought. He seemed to be on the same wavelength, because his next remark was:

'Peter tells me you're the Nostradamus of the bridge world.'

'Not exactly. Nostradamus foretold the death of kings, the downfall of dynasties, things like that. I just believe there's a connection between personality and time of birth.'

'Oh, I thought the whole idea in astrology was to foretell the future.'

'Not in a Cassandra-like way. Astrologers make informed guesses, based on their knowledge of a person's disposition. There's nothing magical in that.'

'Do you mean that from the date of someone's birth you can tell me something about them?'

'I'd want to know the hour and the place as well; then yes, a great deal.'

'It seems far out to me.'

'Does it, indeed?' This was the kind of unthinking dismissive comment that I find particularly annoying. 'Like all men, you treat matters of which you know nothing with lofty disdain. Have you ever thought how vastly more improbable are the assumptions of most popular religions? I suppose it would be news to you that the ancient Egyptians, who were brilliant mathematicians, incorporated astrological insignia on the Temple of Luxor in 1500 BC? That Pythagoras, Plato, Isaac Newton all believed in the influence of the planets on human existence? That the French scientist, Dr Gauquelin, set out to disprove the correlation between birth signs and occupation and found instead that it was conclusively proved? Have you studied the work of Addey and Ravitz? Did you know that . . .'

Rhett had sunk low in his seat with an air of comical dismay. I put my hand on his and said with a smile, 'Sorry, I always go off like that when people try to put astrology down.' At this moment I noticed Elvin standing in the doorway. He marched up to our table and without any preamble said to me: 'What's this? Have you joined the Pot Peddlers' Union?' I hadn't the slightest idea what he was talking about. Rhett just pulled on his cigar and looked blandly over Elvin's shoulder. When neither of us spoke, Elvin stalked off in the direction of the gaming tables.

'What was all that about?' Rhett asked.

'He thought you and I were dining *à deux*. You might have told him that Ross had been with us.'

'Sorry, I didn't know you were Elvin's property,' said Rhett, annoying me still more. When he found out later what had happened, Elvin apologized to me. I told him he ought to apologize to Rhett.

The British team was doing a little better now and had a chance to qualify for the semi-finals. When the last round began the scores were:

America	85
S. Africa	81
Australia	60
India	58
Italy	54
Britain	52
Argentina	49
China	41

Edward Clinton, the captain, explained the position to me: 'America and South Africa are certain to qualify, and one must reckon on Italy beating China in the last round. The critical matches for us are Britain v. Australia and South Africa v. India. We need to beat Australia by 14–6 or better and at the same time to pick up 7 points on India.'

I had intended to kibitz, but Rosanna suggested a shopping trip to Italy in Habib's car. This was too good to miss. I was amused by the way she haggled over everything she bought. 'It's in the blud,' she said, with a hilarious imitation of Hamish MacBride's Glasgow accent.

At one point the conversation took a surprising turn.

'Shoukry won a bomb at blackjack last night,' Rosanna remarked. 'Poor Elvin lost his booties.' (Maurice's theory again: the more you need to win, the less chance you've got.) 'It's a shame about Elvin, isn't it? Shoukry knows all about his money troubles. You know, Toni, Shoukry admires you very much. He'd be very willing to help Elvin.'

For a moment or two I didn't realize what she was saying. The message seemed to be: if I would let Shoukry sweep me off on his camel he would relieve Elvin of his financial worries. Elvin would think that an excellent idea, I was sure. I didn't.

When Rosanna and I arrived at the Sporting Club after a cheerful dinner at the Hotel de Paris, Britain was leading Australia and India was trailing South Africa, so the situation was promising. 'I didn't play Miles and Leonard in the afternoon,' Clinton remarked to Hervey. 'I've put them in now because I mustn't let them think I've lost confidence.'

The hands were flat and at the interval, with just 8 boards to go, Britain was leading Australia 103–68, and South Africa leading India 83–66. If the scores in these matches stayed about the same, Britain would scrape into fourth place behind America, South Africa and Italy.

Edward put in the Scottish pair for the last 8 boards. Miles sat glowering at a small table, drinking on his own. The play on bridgerama was level and when the last board went up it was certain that Britain would win by 17–3, possibly 18–2. But meanwhile news was filtering through that India was gaining hand over fist against South Africa. Leonard went to see what was happening and came back with this alarming report:

'The Africans are throwing the match! There's not the slightest doubt of it.'

Edward quickly explained that the draw for the semi-final would be teams 1 v. 4 from the qualifying round, and 2 v. 3. If the South Africans could push India into third place they would play India in the semi-final, not Italy.

A few minutes later it was all over. Britain had beaten Australia 17–3 and India had beaten South Africa 16–4, just pipping Italy for third place. Britain was out. The score in the last 8 boards of the India-South Africa match had been 44–2 for India.

There was pandemonium when the result was announced. Miles banged a beer-mug on the table, shouting 'Bloody Boers!' (Not that they were Boers, anything but!) Other British supporters joined in. Edward held up his hand and said, 'Hold your horses. We must treat this in a dignified way. I'm going to find the South African captain and tell him formally that we intend to appeal.'

The argument raged for hours in the lobby of the Metropole. The Indians weren't going to admit that their opponents had made them a present of the match. 'No, no, that is all tommy-rot and jolly nonsense,' their captain declared, with a flash of gleaming teeth. 'Lose on purpose, most surely not. Our boys played with incredible courage and boldness at the end. *Kaphar hunu bhanda marnu ramro*,' he cried, waving his fist.

'That's the motto of the Gurkhas,' said Laura unexpectedly. 'It is better to die than live as a coward.'

'By Jove, dear lady, that is absolutely spot-on,' said the Indian captain.

The South African supporters maintained that it was perfectly fair for them to take any lawful action that would improve their own chances. There had been much debate about this at one time in the bridge magazines. Julia, who had played at Wimbledon as a girl, listened in silence for a while, then removed her ebony cigarette-holder and gave us her opinion (which was mine, too): 'In tournaments you always play your best. Anything else is despicable.'

When I went up to our room some time after two in the morning, Hervey was still awake. I told him about the 'tommyrot and jolly nonsense'. He laughed a little weakly and said:

'That's already been settled. There was a committee meeting soon after the match. They said that even if it were certain that South Africa had thrown the match there would be no way to alter the standings. There was some half-assed twaddle about future events being organized differently so that this sort of situation couldn't arise again. Anyway,' he added heavily, 'people will have something else to talk about tomorrow.'

'What's that?'

'John Bassett called me aside during the evening. He's chairman of the Appeals Committee. He wants me to attend a meeting tomorrow morning.'

'What's it all about?'

'It's confidential, I can't tell you yet.'

'For God's sake, Hervey, it's late and I'm tired. Why bring it up at all if you're not going to tell me what it is?'

'For one thing, I've had to order an early breakfast and you'd want to know why. Oh, I suppose it'll be all over the place by the morning. There may be something about it in the Bulletin. I may as well tell you. It's the same old story.'

'What old story?'

'Another cheating accusation. A big one.'

'Not again! Who against?'

'Rosswick and Brindley.'

The Inquiry

by Hervey Pearson

The meeting of the Appeals Committee to inquire into the allegations against Rosswick and Brindley was held on the morning of Wednesday 23 April, the semi-final was due to start the same evening. John Bassett, a Canadian who was chairman of the committee, asked me to call at his office in the Sporting Club before the meeting began.

'Good morning, Hervey,' he said, 'thank you for arriving so early. I wanted to have a word with you before the meeting. You won't be a voting member of the committee, but you could help in two ways. First, as Rosswick is involved, there should be at least one British representative. Second, the proceedings will be recorded and in time there'll be a transcript. You'd be a good man to put this into shape, cutting out the unimportant and repetitive passages.'

I said I'd help in any way I could but as for the editorial job I thought they might find someone better qualified – an English master at school once said my essays were as though someone had turned on the bath-water and forgotten to turn off the tap. John said don't worry about that, the report can be tarted up. 'By the way,' he went on, 'you didn't ask me last night who had brought the accusation.'

'I could see you were very busy.'

'You'll never guess. It was the Chinamen.'

'*Who?*'

'Yes, the Chinks. First time they've qualified for the world championship and they're acting like bloody professionals already. It would be funny if it weren't so sad. Well, Hervey, thank you for your co-operation, I'll see you at the meeting in a few minutes.'

These accusations of cheating have been the bane of the tournament world since about 1950 – somebody once remarked that they were practically an arm of tactics. At first it was mostly about players exchanging hand signals, so diagonal screens were placed across the tables so that players couldn't see their partners – but this made no difference, we had the Americans accusing the Italians of playing footy-footy under the table. Then the Americans turned on one another and alleged a series of significant sniffs and coughs during an international trial. Two years ago the Hungarians insisted on tests to make sure the chairs weren't bugged. None of these allegations were ever proved – or even substantiated to any extent – and I felt pretty sure that it would be the same this time.

The Inquiry was held in a long narrow room. The set-up was like a naval court martial, with a table at one end where the committee sat. At the left there were tables for the woman operating the recording apparatus and for myself. The two counsel sat at card tables right and left of centre, facing the committee; Rosswick and Brindley sat behind their counsel, and the American captain was opposite me. There was a chair for witnesses in the centre.

This is my draft of the proceedings:

MEETING OF THE APPEALS COMMITTEE
HELD AT 9.30 AM ON WEDNESDAY 23 APRIL 1993

Present:

The Appeals Committee	Mr Rudi Vector
Mr John Bassett (chairman)	Mr Harold Garner
M. Claude Varenne	Mr Constantin Sadoveanu
Mr Peter Schwartz	Mr Rhett Brindley
Mr Aswam Khattak	Mr Peter Rosswick
M. Charles de Jouniac	Mr Hervey Pearson
Mr David Hampton (secretary)	Miss Rootjens

MR BASSETT Gentlemen, we are here to inquire into allegations that have been made against Mr Brindley and Mr Rosswick, players in the American team. The allegations were made by Mr Lon Ho, the Chinese delegate, and Mr Wan Pei-Sang, the captain, following the match between these two teams in the second round of the qualifying event.

First, I want to say a word about the functions of everyone present. There are the members of the Appeals Committee. Rudi Vector, the American captain, is naturally present because his team is involved. The American delegate is a member of the committee but will take no part in its deliberations.

We have been fortunate to find among the journalists and officials at this tournament two gentlemen with legal experience who have kindly offered their services. Mr Harold Garner will act on behalf of Mr Brindley and Mr Rosswick and Mr Constantin Sadoveanu will present the case against them. Our friend from England, Mr Hervey Pearson, has undertaken to prepare a transcript of the proceedings. Dave Hampton will perform his usual function as secretary to the committee. Finally, Miss Rootjens is in charge of the recording apparatus.

You may wonder why the Chinese gentlemen are not here to present their case. The reason is that they are already in session with a sub-committee that is studying the bidding and play by the American pair. This sub-committee consists of five experienced Scandinavian players, under the chairmanship of Bertil Hagglof. We will hear their report in due course.

I must tell you how the affair began. Three hours after the match between China and America in the second round on Saturday, Mr Lon Ho requested an interview with representatives of this committee. The Chinese delegate, the

Chinese captain, M. Claude Varenne (the Swiss delegate) and myself met the following morning.

Mr Wan Pei-Sang informed us that both pairs in his team were completely convinced that Mr Brindley and Mr Rosswick had exchanged information in an illegal manner. No code of signals had been intercepted, but the players had made surprising bids and difficult plays with a speed and assurance that was altogether unnatural.

Following procedures that have been laid down for cases of this kind, Claude and I, after consulting with other members of the committee, made arrangements for experienced, professional observers to watch this pair in future matches. As a result of a preliminary report from these observers, it was decided to hold a full Inquiry.

MR GARNER Just a moment, please, Mr Chairman. You seem to imply that the report of these observers created grounds for suspicion against my clients. That is for the whole committee to judge when they have heard whatever evidence is put forward. It is highly prejudicial to say 'As a result of the preliminary report it was decided to hold an inquiry.'

Garner is a dry little stick of a man. He wears half glasses and a bow-tie, and his voice is like a hen scratching on a biscuit-tin. He is of English origin, I believe, though his manner and dress are American – he has a Law practice in Bermuda.

MR BASSETT I put it badly. The situation is simply this: the people concerned have stated that they are ready to report on the observations they have made. I have no idea what they will say.

With the semi-final due to begin this evening, we are very much pressed for time. As soon as the members of the sub-committee are ready to question the American players they will send us a message and either Mr Rosswick or Mr Brindley may decide to leave the present meeting.

Before I call on Mr Sadoveanu to open his case, I want to ask Mr Brindley and Mr Rosswick whether they have any objections to the form of this Inquiry. Mr Brindley?

MR BRINDLEY I'm just plain buffaloed by the whole business. I have heard no evidence, I don't even know what we are supposed to have done. You ask if I have any objections to the form of the Inquiry, my answer is that I object to the whole Inquiry – period.

MR BASSETT Mr Rosswick?

MR ROSSWICK I also have no idea what it's all about. I must say, too, that it seems to me quite wrong for the sub-committee to consist of players who are not familiar with the system that Brindley and I play, nor with our system of signals in defensive play.

MR GARNER I strongly support both those observations. In my submission, there is no justification for holding any Inquiry at all. Whatever the outcome, the reputation of the two players will be damaged for ever. We have seen many examples of this in the past. Players have been vindicated by tribunals but the mud can never be shaken off.

All we have before us are allegations by members of the Chinese team that certain bids and plays made by my clients were incomprehensible to them. Well, I guess the language used by these Chinese gentlemen would be incomprehensible to us, too. The first step, surely, should have been to determine whether a prima facie case had been established.

It is the same in the field of observation. So far – and this is the essential point – there is no case of any kind against my clients. A preliminary court in any part of the world would say they had no case to answer. The composition of the sub-committee therefore becomes a secondary issue, on which I do not need to comment at this time.

MR BASSETT I will not deny that in a legal sense there is some substance in what you say. That is one of the reasons why legal proceedings take such a long time! In the present affair time is a commodity in very short supply. The American team naturally wants to be clear of any imputation before the semi-final begins this evening. I sincerely believe that the best interests of your clients are served by the procedure this committee has adopted. Anything less than an open Inquiry would leave questions unanswered for all time. As chairman I rule that the Inquiry should proceed. Are you ready to open your case, Mr Sadoveanu?

Sadoveanu is a very tall, military-looking Rumanian with a big bushy moustache – you could picture him as a leader of partisans in the mountains. We soon learned that his oratorical style was as flamboyant as his appearance.

MR SADOVEANU My friends, I come before you in the role of prosecutor. That is not my usual role. In Bucharest I am known as Constantin, the defender of the poor and underprivileged. However, without attack there cannot be defence, it is through the operation of opposing forces that we discover the truth. I will play my part as best I can, withdrawing no punches, but with due respect to our American friends I shall not be like those angry gentlemen we see on the films and television who fight every case as a battle that must be won, and who, if they lose, regard the damage to their reputation as a greater tragedy than the misfortune suffered by their hapless clients. My task is simply to present the arguments and evidence in a manner that will enable the court to arrive at the ultimate truth.

Before calling my first witness, I want to say a word about the two classes of evidence in this case. On the one hand there is the internal evidence, based on analysis of the bidding and play as revealed in the hand records. On the other hand there is the observation evidence, relating to the possible exchange of signals. In my view the internal evidence has precedence. Evidence of the eyes can be unreliable, but the hands speak for themselves – they cannot lie.

MR GARNER They can be misinterpreted.

MR SADOVEANU Interpretation is needed in both cases. My point was that the testimony of eye-witnesses, say to a car accident, is less reliable than the film of such an event. We have here the unchallenged record of the bids and plays actually made. If Mr Hagglof's committee says in effect 'No evidence', I shall invite you to find for the defendants on that alone, no matter what evidence is given by the observation witnesses. I think it fair to remark, however, that unlike the witnesses in some previous cases of this kind the observers are from outside. They have – what is the English phrase – thank you, no axe to grind.

MR GARNER It is quite improper to suggest that these observers are more or less deserving of credence than any other witness. They may be tempted to show how clever and perceptive they have been.

MR BASSETT Yes, you must allow the committee to form its own opinion about the credibility of the witnesses, Mr Sadoveanu. Are you ready now to call your first witness?

MR SADOVEANU I call Mr George Emhardt.

This Emhardt I know quite well as 'George' in charge of equipment – I did not know he had other duties, but he could easily be a detective or ex-policeman.

MR SADOVEANU Will you tell us, please, what your duties are at this tournament and by whom you are employed?

MR EMHARDT I am employed by the American Contract Bridge League both as a security officer and as equipment officer.

MR SADOVEANU How were you brought into this affair?

MR EMHARDT On Sunday afternoon I had a call from Mr Bassett, asking me to go to his room. Mr Varenne was there too. They told me that a pair was suspected of exchanging signals. I am experienced in inquiries of this sort. Time being short, and also because Mr Brindley knows me well by sight, I suggested we ought to obtain outside assistance. Mr Bassett told me to go ahead.

I contacted Monsieur Noël Lafitte, the director of a detective agency in this town. He put three of his staff at my disposal. They began their observations on the following afternoon.

MR SADOVEANU Did you make any further report to Mr Bassett?

MR EMHARDT Yes. Early on Tuesday afternoon I informed him that the office staff of the agency had certain findings to report. Mr Bassett said he did not wish to hear details at this stage and instructed me to continue observation.

MR SADOVEANU These three operatives are here to give evidence?

MR EMHARDT Yes. I should mention that Monsieur Lafitte prefers his staff to be anonymous. They are known as Monsieur François, Monsieur Christophe, and Mr Joe, who is English.

MR SADOVEANU Thank you. Now Mr Garner may have some questions for you.

MR GARNER Mr Emhardt, you and I have known one another for many years, but this is the first time I realized you were a bridge player.

MR EMHARDT I haven't said I was a bridge player, Mr Garner.

MR GARNER No, you haven't, have you? You are just an expert who can judge when players are exchanging signals, not a bridge player at all, is that it?

MR EMHARDT I know what the game is about and the sort of thing that goes on. In the way of exchanging messages, that is.

MR GARNER What sort of messages are these?

MR EMHARDT I can only speak from experience of cases in which I have been concerned. Players — not top-class players, I agree — have been detected in attempts to exchange information about the number of honour cards they held — known as points, I believe — and in the play there have been signals asking for the play of a particular suit.

MR GARNER Would you say that information about the club suit was more or less valuable than information about the spade suit?

MR BASSETT The witness has made it quite clear that he does not pose as a bridge expert.

MR GARNER I know, and my point is that this witness — and the same is true, I imagine, of the employees of this detective agency — is quite incapable of assessing the quality and value of information passed by one bridge player to another.

MR BASSETT (to Mr Sadoveanu) Do you wish to re-examine?

MR SADOVEANU Just one question. You have told us that you are familiar with the game of bridge only in the broadest sense.

What do you look for, then, when you conduct your observation of any two players?

MR EMHARDT It may be only one player. I look for variations in the pattern of behaviour and I record the exact moment, in the bidding or play, when the variation occurred. For example, I might make a note that after six cards had been played on a particular deal the player moved his hand across his brow.

MR SADOVEANU And it is for the bridge experts to look for any possible connection between the gesture and the situation confronting the players? Exactly. Thank you, that is all. Mr Hampton, will you kindly call Monsieur François?

This François was a typical inquiry agent, I should imagine, very ordinary-looking, with mousey hair, slightly receding chin, fair colouring, medium height and build.

M. FRANÇOIS Gentlemen, I understand fairly well the English language, but with your permission I will first read a statement which has been prepared by a member of our staff from my notes, which of course were in French.

I am employed by the agency of Monsieur Lafitte. At 10 am on Monday 21 April I received a message at my home instructing me to proceed to the office of Mr Emhardt at the Sporting Club. Two of my colleagues arrived later. We were instructed to observe the two gentlemen whom I see over there and determine whether they were exchanging signals during the play of cards. We watched them play throughout Monday afternoon and part of Monday evening, and again on Tuesday afternoon and evening.

I sat on one of the benches facing the American gentleman with the reddish hair, and my colleague, Christophe, sat opposite the other gentleman. Using concealed cameras, we photographed the two players from the moment they picked up their cards on each deal until the end of play. Film was sent by messenger to our office, and staff there worked throughout the night, analysing every movement made by the players.

Christophe and I examined the film each morning and discussed it with our colleagues. Two variations in behaviour attracted our attention. Both players had the custom, soon after picking up their cards, of looking at the scoresheet on which they had entered the result of the previous deal, and quite often they touched the scorepad or made a mark on it. That was one action we noted. Secondly, as you gentlemen will know, the calls are not spoken but are indicated by the pressing of a button on a sort of dial in the centre of the table. This was not done in a uniform manner. Both players usually pressed the button with the first or index finger, but sometimes they used the second or big finger.

After each period of play certain sheets were brought to the office by Mr Emhardt, which contained records of the cards held by the players. The variations I have just described and the records of the cards actually held by the players were fed into a computer. The object was to discover whether there was any correlation between behaviour patterns and card holdings.

At this point there was a knock on the door, and one of the office staff came in with a message that was handed to the chairman. Before the door closed I heard a hum of conversation – the pressmen were gathering.

John Bassett announced that Mr Hagglof's committee was ready to interview the players. He suggested they might prefer to wait till M. François had finished his evidence, but Brindley stood up and said 'No sweat, I'll go' and walked out.

MR BASSETT (to the witness) Are you able to give us first-hand evidence about the result of this computer test?
M. FRANÇOIS A report was prepared and signed by Monsieur Lafitte. I have copies with me.
MR BASSETT I see, thank you. I think we might break off for ten minutes now while we study Agence Lafitte's report.

Report No. 1
Film taken of Mr Rosswick and Mr Brindley in play extended

over 96 deals. Two noticeable variations in the pattern of behaviour are revealed:

(a) On a minority of occasions either one or both of the players touched, or wrote on, his scorepad after he had picked up his cards for a new deal. This happened on 37 occasions. Of those 37 occasions, the player held fewer than 10 points (counting 4 for an ace, 3 for a king, 2 for a queen, 1 for a jack) 27 times. Since 10 points is the average holding, the proportion of 27 out of 37 is unexpectedly high.

Possible conclusion: That a player who made this gesture was indicating a hand of less than average value.

(b) When indicating a bid by pressing a button on the centre dial, the players generally used the first finger, but sometimes the second finger. Between them, the players used their second finger when making their first call on 55 occasions, and on 25 of those occasions the player's distribution was either 4-4-3-2 or 5-3-3-2. As there are about 20 possible distributions, not counting those which include a suit of eight cards or more, this proportion of 25 out of 55 for two particular distributions appears abnormally high.

Possible conclusion: That the use of the second finger when making the first call was associated with the two distributions, 4-4-3-2 or 5-3-3-2.

The evidence on which this Report is based can be inspected at this office.

Noël Lafitte (Director)

When I read the Report I glanced at Rosswick. He had been sitting with a glassy expression but was now looking quite animated. He was writing notes and passing them to Garner, who nodded as though well satisfied.

MR BASSETT (to Mr Sadoveanu) Do you wish to examine the witness on the contents of this Report?

MR SADOVEANU It appears that on 27 occasions out of 37 when a player touched his scorepad, he held less than an average hand. The normal expectation, obviously, would be 18 or 19 times. Would you agree, Monsieur François, that the result obtained was most improbable, like tossing a coin 37 times and finding that it turned up heads 27 times?

MR GARNER The witness is not a statistician.

MR SADOVEANU He has produced this Report and I am asking him to confirm its contents. Secondly, on 25 occasions out of 55 when a player making his first call pressed the button with his second finger he held either 4-4-3-2 or 5-3-3-2 distribution; that is, one or other of two hand patterns out of 20. Is that right?

M. FRANÇOIS That is exact.

MR SADOVEANU Thank you. Your witness.

MR GARNER Monsieur François, are you familiar with the story of the mountain that laboured to produce a mouse?

M. FRANÇOIS I do not quite understand those words in connection with this affair.

MR GARNER Then let me explain. Your agency has expended goodness knows how many man hours in obtaining this evidence and has come up with two items that could scarcely be more trivial or unpersuasive. You say that this touching of the scorepad occurred especially when the player held a hand of less than average value?

M. FRANÇOIS The Report appears to say that, yes.

MR GARNER Surely a player who holds a poor hand is more likely to let his attention wander to the previous deal than a player with a strong hand?

M. FRANÇOIS I am not familiar with the habits of bridge players.

MR GARNER The members of this committee will understand well enough the point I am making. Now let me ask you this: the Report states that a certain gesture was made on 37 occasions and that on 27 of these a player held a poor hand: what happened on the other 10 occasions?

M. FRANÇOIS Nothing special was observed.

MR GARNER If we adopt your hypothesis that to indicate a weak hand a player would touch his scorepad, would this not be done on all occasions? Such a code is useless if not practised consistently. Otherwise, how can the players rely on one another to be giving the right signal?

M. FRANÇOIS It is not easy for me to answer these questions. The Report simply describes what was observed.

MR GARNER No, my friend, the Report does more than that. It invites the reader to draw certain very dubious conclusions. Now let me turn to the second item. It was suggested that the use of the second finger to press the button appeared to correspond with the holding of 4-4-3-2 or 5-3-3-2 distribution. Are you aware that the hand patterns quoted are by far the commonest and have between them a frequency of 38 per cent? In the light of that, the proportion you quote, 25 out of 55, is not in the least remarkable, is it?

MR SADOVEANU The witness is not a statistician.

MR GARNER I am simply inviting him to use his commonsense. I suggest further that the whole method of identifying a particular gesture and relating it to some type of card-holding is full of pitfalls. As we are in Monte Carlo, let me give you a homely illustration. You might find at one table in the casino that black was having a great run, at another red was outstripping black. You will arrive at different answers depending on when and where you conduct your observation. In the present case, Monsieur François, if you had studied some other quirk of behaviour you might have come up with quite different answers.

MR BASSETT You are entering the realms of argument, dealing with questions that are not within the competence of this witness. I think we should leave this subject until we have the whole picture. It would be convenient if we could hear the other witnesses from Agence Lafitte before we adjourn for lunch.

MR SADOVEANU I call Monsieur Christophe.

Christophe was a dapper little man, very Gallic, with dark brown hair parted in the middle and plastered down on either side of his forehead.

MR SADOVEANU Monsieur Christophe, we have heard from your colleague the part you played in observing and photographing the two players. Have you anything further to add?

M. CHRISTOPHE Yes. I am not speaking well English. If you permit, I will read from a paper I have:
I am an expert in electronic communication. It was decided to test whether the two players might be exchanging messages with the aid of an electronic device. Such a device could be concealed in the shoe of one player, or in a pocket, and his partner could receive impulses from a receiver on some part of his body. I conducted a test to determine whether any metal was concealed on the body of either person. The test for Monsieur Rosswick was positive.

MR SADOVEANU Could something quite innocent, such as a keyring, a *porte-clefs*, have caused this?

M. CHRISTOPHE I am not thinking so. He carry a sporting shirt.

MR SADOVEANU He was wearing a sports shirt? And somewhere on his person there was a metal that gave a positive reaction to your test? Thank you.

MR GARNER You are saying, not that there was actual evidence of electronic communication, but that there was a theoretical possibility?

M. CHRISTOPHE (after translation) Yes, not certain.

MR GARNER Might a gold tooth, for example, produce a reaction?

M. CHRISTOPHE (after translation) It is possible.

MR GARNER Mr Rosswick has a gold tooth. Would you like him to show it to you?

MR BASSETT Mr Rosswick is not a horse to be inspected. We will take his word for it. There is one more observation witness to hear, I believe?

Rounds one and two had gone to the defence, there wasn't much doubt of that. Garner had dealt adequately with François and the business about the electronic gadget had been a fiasco. The next witness, Joe, was a big chap with a ruddy complexion, more like a meat porter than a detective.

MR SADOVEANU Mr Joe, will you tell us from the beginning how you came to be involved in this affair?

MR JOE From the beginning, eh? Monday morning, it was. You don't get many plummy jobs in this business but I had one of the best, lying on the beach in the sunshine, keeping observation on a certain party whose husband ... well, you don't want to know about that, do you? Anyway, there I was, watching the birds, and I don't mean the kind that flies, when I hear my name called. It was a young chap from the office, speaks English, 'On your feet,' he says, 'you're wanted back at the ranch, I'll take over your job.' 'That you won't, young feller-me-lad,' I said, 'you've got a taxi waiting, I'll bet on that, off we go.' Back at the office the boss and me and one of the Monsewers had a bit of a confab, then the Monsewer and I went along to the Sporting Club and met friend George here. George says, 'These two lads may be up to something, stick around and see what you can pick up.' What he meant was, bug their rooms, but bugging's against the law of the land in this town, my boss wouldn't allow it. But there's nothing to stop a fellow using a hearing aid, is there, even one that's a bit special.

I followed these two around whenever I could and I also had the job of watching them at the table to see if I could pick up anything the cameras might be missing. I didn't see anything there, but I did pick up one or two bits of conversation that sounded suspicious. Then on Tuesday ...

MR GARNER Please refrain from dropping hints. If you heard any remark you considered suspicious, let us know what it was. It is possible, after all, that you are not familiar with the idioms that bridge players use.

MR JOE All right, guv'nor, forget what I said, I'll come to the meat of it. Tuesday morning, these two lads were having a late breakfast in the coffee shop. I sat at a table too far away for normal hearing, you get me, but with my machine I could hear every word they spoke. And one of them, the American it was, said this: 'Pete, we've got to change the system. They've begun to cotton on.'

MR SADOVEANU 'Pete, we've got to change the system. They've begun to cotton on.' What exactly does the phrase 'cotton on' mean?

MR JOE Catch the meaning, like.

MR SADOVEANU Thank you, I wanted to be sure. 'Pete, we've got to change the system. They've begun to cotton on.' Those were the exact words? You are absolutely sure?

MR JOE Sure I'm sure. I wrote them down at once. Here's my book, you can see.

MR SADOVEANU I think we ought all to look at your book.

MR BASSETT That's not necessary. Mr Garner?

MR GARNER You've been the fly on the wall, Joe?

MR JOE Fly on the . . . Oh, I get it. Very neat. Yes.

MR GARNER Rather a large fly?

MR JOE Some big chaps can be very quiet and some small chaps can make a lot of noise.

MR GARNER Would it surprise you to know that my clients were well aware of your presence during the last two days? That Mr Brindley wondered when you were going to be so bold as to ask for their autographs?

MR BASSETT Don't tease the witness, Harold. Come to the point.

MR GARNER Oh, I thought I had made my point. The witness was not, as he seems to have thought, an invisible man, well placed to overhear secrets. My clients tell me they knew he was around. I will have something to say later about the propriety of eavesdropping with the aid of a mechanical contrivance. We will turn now to the remark to which so much significance has been attached. 'We'll have to change the system, they've begun to cotton on.' What do you think the word 'system' means for bridge players?

MR JOE Same as it does for anyone else, so far as I know: a sort of scheme or arrangement.

MR GARNER And you, who know little or nothing about this game, concluded that the scheme or arrangement was a guilty one?

MR JOE It sounded that way.

MR GARNER Sounded? Does this machine of yours record the

decibels? Did Mr Brindley lower his voice to a conspiratorial whisper, like the wicked squire in a pantomime?

MR JOE I didn't mean it that way. I meant that the words 'cotton on' had a sort of secret ring about them.

MR GARNER But now I have asked you whether Brindley spoke these words in a subdued, conspiratorial way?

MR JOE Not that I remember. But as I have said, I wasn't close, he wouldn't have known I could overhear.

MR GARNER The coffee-shop where this conversation took place has back-to-back compartments, has it not? For all my clients knew, there might have been someone a couple of feet away from them, isn't that so?

MR JOE It was late, mid-morning, the place was more or less empty.

MR GARNER That's not an answer to my question, but we'll leave it there. The word 'system': will you take it from me that this word has a specialized meaning in bridge? That systems of bidding and systems of defensive play are the subject of endless discussion?

MR JOE If you say so.

MR GARNER There are numerous ways in which players may signal to one another in a perfectly lawful way. For example, the play of an odd or even card may in some circumstances convey a message, and this would be known as a system of defensive play. However, the point may come where they feel that the message is of more value to an opponent than to partner. They may then decide to change the system. Do you understand?

MR JOE Just about.

MR GARNER Viewed in that light, is there anything in the least suspicious in a player saying in effect to his partner, 'I think we ought to change our system. The opponents are picking up our signals and turning them to their own advantage'?

MR JOE This is getting beyond me. I have told you the words that were spoken, it is for you experts to interpret them.

MR GARNER I have no more questions.

MR SADOVEANU Mr Garner has explained to you, quite fairly,

that bridge players use systems in both bidding and play and these are a frequent subject for discussion. He did not, however, make it totally evident that these systems, or signals, have to be announced to the opponents. Secret systems or arrangements of any kind are strictly forbidden and amount to cheating. Now remember the words 'They've begun to cotton on'; could they refer to a perfectly legal and open system of signalling?

MR GARNER Objection! Only a moment ago the witness said himself that he was not qualified to interpret the words that were spoken. If you wish, my clients will explain the context of the remark that is causing so much fuss.

MR BASSETT It might be better to leave this whole matter until the players themselves give their evidence. There is no point in continuing the argument while the present witness is on the stand. Thank you, Joe, I hope you will be able to return to the pleasant occupation from which you were summoned.

We will break for lunch now and resume at 2.15. Please do not discuss the proceedings at this Inquiry even with one another. I will make a short statement to keep the press at bay. Dave, will you check that no notes or documents are left lying around? And please ask Mr Hagglof to be available early in the afternoon.

MR HAMPTON John, you haven't forgotten Mrs Burton, have you? I did tell you that I had a telephone call early this morning from a Mrs Burton, who said she had read in the Bulletin that there was to be a meeting of the Appeals Committee and thought she might be able to help.

MR BASSETT Anyone know a Mrs Burton? No one? Well, we'll have to fix her in somewhere before the closing speeches.

MR HAMPTON And, John, just before we resumed after the coffee break, Elvin Starr spoke to me. He wants to give evidence, too.

MR BASSETT We all know Elvin Starr. I suppose ... No, we will take him first. Ask him to be available at 2.15, will you, Dave?

There was a crowd of pressmen outside. I evaded them as politely as I could and took the lift to my room. Toni was there.

'How's it going?' she asked.

'Even Steven, I'd say. In the end it's going to depend on the hands themselves.'

'How's Ross bearing up?'

'He doesn't look well. Order some coffee and sandwiches, will you?' I slumped into a chair. 'It's like a bear-pit downstairs. I could do with a rest.'

After Toni had ordered, I asked her about Elvin. 'We've been told that Elvin's going to give evidence. What's he going to say?'

'How should I know?'

'How should you know? He's been following you round like a poodle for the past six months; I don't suppose he has many secrets from you.'

'All I can tell you is that when I was on the balcony this morning I could hear a violent argument going on between Elvin and Maurice and Shoukry. Old moneybags, as you call him, said to Maurice at one point, "I thought you knew better by now than to cross me". And whether you believe it or not, I like Elvin. At least he's sincere and doesn't go round putting on a permanent act.'

'If anyone puts on an act, it's you. And Elvin sincere! You told me yourself he was in a vile temper after he had played against Rosswick and Brindley, and now he's proposing to give evidence for them.'

'Who said he was going to give evidence *for* them?'

When John Bassett opened the afternoon session he made the same mistake that I had done.

MR BASSETT The programme for this afternoon, gentlemen, is that we take Elvin Starr first and then the report from the sub-committee, which I understand is being prepared at this moment. It is, of course, normal practice to hear all the evidence from one side in a continuous line, but the evidence of the sub-committee comes into a different category from the remainder and that is why we are going to take all the individual witnesses first. Have you any idea, Harold, what Elvin is going to say and how long his evidence is likely to take?

MR GARNER I know nothing about it. He hasn't spoken to me nor to my clients.

MR HAMPTON Er, John, are you quite sure that Elvin is a defence witness? When he spoke to me during the morning break he was in the middle of a conversation with one of the Chinese players.

MR BASSETT Oh! Do you know anything about this, Hervey?

MR PEARSON Nothing definite. But from something that was said to me, I think Dave may be right.

MR BASSETT We'd better have him in and find out.

Elvin – looking quite smart for him, in navy-blue trousers, a yellow shirt, and a Gucci scarf – strode in and took the witness's chair without a glance at Rosswick and Brindley.

MR SADOVEANU Mr Starr, as I expect you know, I have been assigned the role of prosecutor in this unhappy affair. We have been told that your evidence will support that of the Chinese players who originally brought the charge against Mr Rosswick and Mr Brindley. Is that correct?

MR STARR Yes.

MR SADOVEANU At what stage were your suspicions first aroused?

MR STARR Quite early in the second half of the match we played against America in the third round.

MR SADOVEANU Did you know then that the Chinese players had already made a complaint to the Chairman of the Appeals Committee?

MR STARR No. I knew nothing at all about that.

MR SADOVEANU Your suspicions were formed quite independently, then?

MR BASSETT He has just said so.

MR SADOVEANU Perhaps we had better hear Mr Starr's story from the beginning.

MR STARR Early in the second half I was the declarer in two close contracts, one of three clubs and one of four spades. In each case the defence was good and smoothly played. There is nothing remarkable in that, but I was not comfortable. When opponents make difficult plays with very little thought, I notice and I tend to be suspicious. My phrase for it is that there was an unnatural time structure. To explain what I mean, I want to show you board 19, the one I played in four spades. I have copies here of the relevant hand record.

MR GARNER Objection! An independent sub-committee has been appointed to examine the internal evidence from the match against China. If this witness is permitted to introduce a hand from another match, my clients must be allowed to present other hands from other matches and we won't finish this Inquiry for another week.

MR BASSETT If Mr Starr has come to give evidence about a particular deal, I think we ought to hear what he has to say. You will be able to cross-examine him, and in your final address to make whatever point you wish about the value of a single example.

Dave Hampton passed round copies of the hand, which was as follows:

Dealer, East   Both sides vulnerable

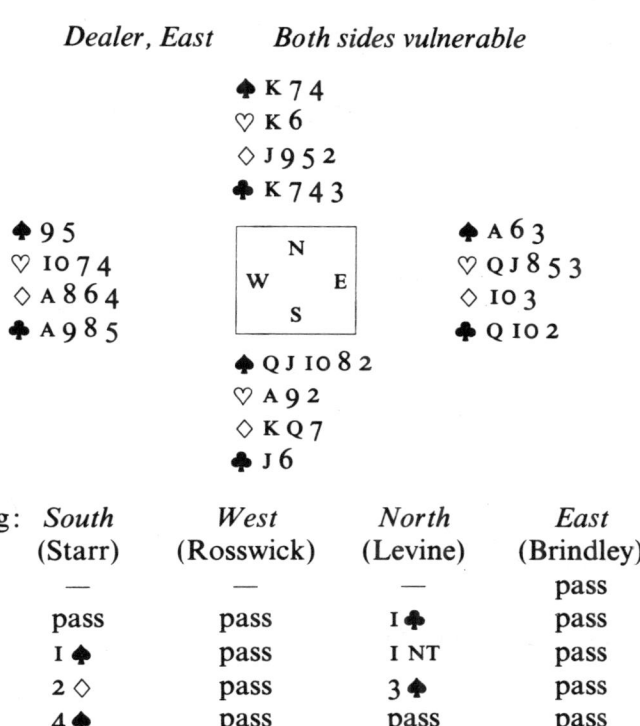

Bidding:	South (Starr)	West (Rosswick)	North (Levine)	East (Brindley)
	—	—	—	pass
	pass	pass	1♣	pass
	1♠	pass	1 NT	pass
	2◊	pass	3♠	pass
	4♠	pass	pass	pass

Final contract – Four Spades

MR STARR I will explain the bidding briefly. I was South, and in the Habibi Heart system a pass in first or second position indicates the values for an opening bid. The partner of the player who has made a 'strong pass' is obliged to open, with rare exceptions, and here North's one club showed moderate values – 8-11 points with no 4-card major. South's one spade promised a 5-card suit, North's one no-trump was forcing, and South, lacking a second suit, had to bid his lowest 3-card suit. The rest was natural.

Rosswick, who was West, led the ace of clubs and switched immediately to a low diamond – not the most obvious play in the world. When East came in with the ace of trumps he led his second diamond and obtained a ruff to beat the contract.

MR SADOVEANU In your opinion, was this lead of the low diamond at trick two a play that could scarcely have been made without the aid of illegal information?

MR GARNER The witness is quite capable of expressing his opinion without the aid of any prompting.

MR SADOVEANU I thought the conclusion was obvious, but I will re-phrase the question. What opinion did you form about this unhesitating lead of the low diamond at trick two?

MR STARR As you can see, West held four diamonds to the ace, there were four diamonds in dummy, and I had bid diamonds. West had a problem – whether to lead ace and another, which would be best if East held a singleton diamond, or to play his partner for a doubleton diamond and a fast trick in trumps. It was out of this world to lead the low diamond without any apparent consideration.

MR SADOVEANU What was your state of mind after this hand had been played?

MR STARR I was very much on my guard and from then on I kept my eyes open.

MR SADOVEANU Did you observe anything else?

MR STARR Yes. I had a strong impression that some communication was taking place before the first round of bidding was completed. Again, it was a question of tempo. Sometimes there were pauses for which there could be no logical explanation.

MR SADOVEANU Do you mean that they sometimes took an unnaturally long time to make a perfectly obvious call, such as a pass when there could be nothing to think about?

MR STARR The pauses were more noticeable when they were intending to bid. It was as though they were assimilating and assessing some extra information.

MR SADOVEANU So what was your final conclusion?

MR STARR I was convinced that something was going on. I am not normally suspicious and I very seldom make suggestions of this sort.

MR SADOVEANU I see. Thank you.

MR BASSETT Harold, I expect you would like to consult with your clients before cross-examining?

Garner, Rosswick and Brindley conferred at the other end of the room for ten minutes — I noticed that Rosswick did most of the talking — then Garner began his cross-examination:

MR GARNER Mr Starr, you say that at the end of the match you were convinced that something was going on, as you put it. I presume you reported this to your captain?

MR STARR I had a discussion with my partner, but no, I didn't make a formal protest to my captain.

MR GARNER What! Here you were, playing a vital match in the world championship; you were convinced your opponents were cheating, and you did nothing about it?

MR STARR I am not in the habit of bandying accusations that cannot be conclusively proved. Brindley does that, I don't.

MR BASSETT Please try to avoid comments of a personal nature.

MR GARNER I was just about to ask you about your relationship with my clients. When you were in America last year you played in a team with Mr Brindley and Mr Rosswick, did you not? You had some disagreements, I believe?

MR STARR I didn't care for some of their friends, that was all. We didn't have anything you could call a quarrel.

MR GARNER And this week, what have your relations been with the two players?

MR STARR Normal.

MR GARNER I want to ask you some questions about that. On your last night in America did you play in a poker game and lose more than you were able to pay at the time?

MR STARR Yes.

MR GARNER And did Mr Rosswick save you considerable embarrassment by paying out on your behalf?

MR STARR Yes.

MR GARNER Mr Rosswick informs me that when a few days ago he asked you to settle up you were extremely short with him. Is that a fair comment?

MR STARR He approached me at a very inconvenient moment, when I had been losing at the casino.

MR GARNER And you have not so far repaid him?

MR STARR No.

MR SADOVEANU 'For loan oft loses both itself and friend'.

MR GARNER I am much obliged to my friend. A most apt quotation. Now I am going to refer to another incident. When Mr Brindley was dining with a lady at Loews Hotel earlier this week, did you approach their table and for no reason whatsoever make a most offensive comment?

MR STARR There was a misunderstanding. I apologized to both of them later.

MR GARNER Are you asking us to believe that, despite these two incidents, relations between yourself and my clients were, as you said, normal?

MR STARR The incidents you have referred to had no connection whatsoever with the evidence I have given.

MR GARNER So you say. But whatever your personal feelings, this was a needle match, was it not, Britain v. America?

MR STARR It was an important match, obviously.

MR GARNER A match you were particularly keen to win?

MR STARR For the reason I have given you: it was likely to be a critical match for our team, which had made a poor start.

MR GARNER But the match went badly for you from the beginning, did it not?

MR STARR The first half was level, the second half was a landslide.

MR GARNER I am not going to suggest that disappointment at the way the match was going was responsible for your suspicions. But I do suggest that for various reasons you were unusually tense and that this may have affected your judgement?

MR STARR Not in the least.

MR GARNER Not keyed-up? All right, we will leave that. Now, this hand you brought to our notice. You have not been entirely frank with this committee, have you?

MR STARR What do you mean?

MR GARNER I mean that you failed to draw the committee's attention to at least one very relevant point. The original pass and the opening one club were part of the Habibi Heart system, but from then on your use of the 5-card major, the forcing response of one notrump, and the rebid of a 3-card minor — all this was part of a style of bidding which Mr Rosswick plays himself, was it not?

MR STARR I believe so, yes.

MR GARNER So he would have been fully prepared for the rebid of two diamonds on a 3-card suit?

MR STARR He would know it was possible.

MR GARNER Mr Rosswick says further that you considered for a moment or two before rebidding two diamonds and that he formed the impression you were wondering whether to bid two spades on a very fair 5-card suit or to bid the 3-card minor.

MR STARR It is easy to say that when you see the full hand.

MR GARNER Come now, that is a most unworthy reply.

MR STARR I don't remember that I hesitated at all. Two diamonds is the system bid.

MR GARNER Mr Rosswick maintains nevertheless that he formed the opinion during the bidding that you had only three diamonds and this opinion was strengthened when he saw the four diamonds in dummy. Now let us look closely at West's problem after he had led the ace of clubs and his partner had played the 2. Mr Rosswick says that he and his partner play 'count signals' and that since his partner would have played high-low with an even number of clubs he could place him with precisely three clubs. Do you accept that?

MR STARR Yes.

MR GARNER Since you did not rebid the spades, as you would have done with six, your distribution had to be 5-2-4-2 or 5-3-3-2. Do you agree with that?

MR STARR There are other possibilities, such as 5-1-5-2, but I agree these were the likely alternatives.

MR GARNER And since 5-3-3-2 is a much commoner distribution than 5-4-2-2, it was perfectly logical for Rosswick to play you for three diamonds, quite apart from the special inference I mentioned earlier?

MR STARR I don't dispute that. I say only that no player would lead the low diamond at trick two without giving the matter some consideration. It is not just a matter of whether partner has a doubleton or singleton diamond: for the low diamond to achieve anything, partner must have a fast trick in trumps and there is no reason to place him with the ace of trumps.

MR GARNER The low diamond would also be a winning play if partner held Kx, would it not?

MR STARR Yes, you can put that in as makeweight on your side.

MR GARNER Now, this question of tempo on which you have laid so much stress: suppose for a moment that we accept your hypothesis that the players were exchanging information in an illegal manner and that Rosswick somehow knew his partner held a doubleton and not a singleton diamond: is there any reason why he should not still pause awhile before making the critical play?

MR STARR If he was cool and collected, no; but I formed the impression that Rosswick was in a highly nervous state, incapable of dispassionate analysis.

MR GARNER Capable, however, of defeating your team by a substantial margin. You used the phrase 'unnatural time structure'. Bit vague, isn't it? Not a very firm peg on which to hang an accusation of this gravity?

MR STARR Let me put it this way: a doctor, with his experience, may diagnose an illness from instinct rather than from recognizable symptoms. In the same way, as an experienced player, I can sense when the pair I am playing against are not straight.

MR GARNER So your case is that you had some sort of inner knowledge. That doesn't impress me and I doubt if it will impress the members of this committee. (Don't stand up, Constantin, I'm sorry, that was improper comment and I withdraw it.) Finally, you say that you sensed some irregularity in the way the players made their initial calls?

MR STARR Again, the tempo was unnatural. It was as though they were waiting for some information before they made their first bid.

MR GARNER Is it not correct to take a few moments before making a call, however obvious?

MR STARR It is correct to bid with a consistent rhythm, which is what they failed to do.

MR GARNER Having formed the conclusions that you say you did, what steps did you take to obtain further evidence? Did you watch Rosswick and Brindley in other matches to see if you could gain more information about this suspected code?

MR STARR No, it would have been a slow business and probably would not have helped. You have to be at the table to get the feel of these things.

MR GARNER If it had not been for the complaint made by the team from China, we would never have heard from you in this matter?

MR STARR As I said earlier, I did not have the sort of evidence that could be put before a committee without further support.

MR GARNER I agree with you there! All we have heard is that you had vague feelings of uneasiness. Sometimes the players acted too quickly for your liking, sometimes too slowly. I have no further questions.

At first it had seemed pretty damning when a player of Elvin's stature gave evidence against his former team-mates, but Garner had managed the cross-examination very cleverly, I thought, making Elvin appear prejudiced and his evidence shallow. However Sadoveanu recovered some ground in re-examination.

MR SADOVEANU If there is something I have overlooked I am sure you will tell me, but one point did puzzle me about West's construction of the South hand. You said, or at least you agreed with Mr Garner, that the main possibilities were 5-2-4-2 or 5-3-3-2. But might not South have held 5-1-4-3 or 5-3-4-1 distribution? Would he not then also have rebid two diamonds?

MR STARR Yes, but the assumption was made, you remember, that East's 2 of clubs on the first trick placed him with three clubs and therefore South with two. Thus 5-4-3-1 is ruled out.

However, now I come to think of it, East could have held Q2 alone and South 10 xx.

MR SADOVEANU So in this last case South could have held 5-1-4-3 distribution? I am glad the point I raised was not entirely misconceived. Having heard Mr Garner's comments, what is your opinion now about the lead of the low diamond at trick two?

MR STARR Mr Garner's point that East might hold K x of diamonds was a valid one, though not important. My view of the matter is very clear: the lead of the low diamond was against the odds, and the unhesitating lead of a low diamond was not open to any innocent explanation.

MR SADOVEANU Finally, the suggestion that from the first you had hostile feelings towards Mr Brindley and Mr Rosswick: is there any truth in that?

MR STARR None at all. As a matter of fact, on the morning of the match between Britain and America I had a date to play in a tennis match against Brindley and his partner.

MR SADOVEANU And were there any fireworks in this game?

MR STARR No, it was rained off.

The next witness was Bertil Hagglof, a tall, fair man with a hawkish nose – he is editor of a magazine and often visits England. He was carrying a sheaf of papers.

MR BASSETT Will you take this chair, Bertil? I think you know everyone. While Dave is handing round the report of your committee, perhaps you could give us the sequence of events from your side?

MR HAGGLOF You first spoke to me about this affair, Mr Chairman, yesterday morning. During the day I found four people to complete the sub-committee. They are all Scandinavians, understanding both Swedish and English – and, of course, bridge. I asked them to say nothing to anyone and to be ready to meet at 9.30 this morning.

I thought it would save time if during the evening I had a talk with the Chinese players who had brought the accusation. Mr Wan Pei Sang and one of his players, Mr Robert

Wch (which is rather difficult to pronounce), came to my room and we spent about two hours going through the hands that had disturbed the Chinese players.

I know quite well the systems and conventions used by the American players, and I was able to suggest that three deals which were in Mr Wan's list should be withdrawn. The Chinese gentlemen, having heard my comments and explanations, were in full agreement. There remained seven examples – either bids, leads or plays – requiring fuller examination.

My committee studied these hands this morning. One of the lead problems was struck out, as some members of the committee thought the player's choice was understandable. At about mid-day, as you know, we requested the attendance of one of the players. Mr Brindley spent over an hour with us. After further discussion I drafted the report which you have now.

MR BASSETT Thank you, that is most helpful. It will take us a little time to master the contents of your report, so I suggest we adjourn for fifteen minutes or so. I asked for a waiter to be ready with pots of coffee, so we may be lucky.

The report was not long – it listed five occasions where the bidding or play gave rise to suspicion, one of the original six being withdrawn because the committee had accepted the player's explanation. In two instances the verdict was 'not conclusive in itself but giving ground for suspicion when compared with other hands where a similar sequence occurred'; one bidding sequence was marked 'giving grounds for suspicion of a private understanding'; and two play hands had the comment 'committee not satisfied with the player's explanation'. The report concluded with this summary:

Mr Rosswick and Mr Brindley played 32 boards out of 48 in the match against China. About ten of the hands were closely scrutinized, but for purposes of comparison the committee looked at all deals where this pair was active.

It would have been helpful if the records of other matches in the qualifying round had been studied, but there was no time for this to be done. In the committee's opinion the bidding and play of this pair is consistent with the exchange of unlawful information, but the sample is too small for any definite conclusion to be drawn from this type of evidence alone.

The impression one gathered from this report was that the committee thought the players were probably guilty but lacked sufficient evidence to say so outright. I noticed too that Hagglof avoided looking at the two players. After everyone had studied the report John called the meeting to order and addressed Hagglof.

MR BASSETT Quite rightly, in this report, you have included the technical details of the hands that were the subject of your discussions. Mr Sadoveanu and Mr Garner will put questions to you about the report, but from the chair I must bar any questions of a technical nature. Otherwise everyone will want to join in and there will be no end to our deliberations. What is that Latin proverb – something *homines* – thank you, Constantin, *quot homines tot sententiae*, meaning that there are as many opinions as there are people. Certainly that is true when bridge bidding and play are being argued. So nothing technical, please. You will bear that in mind, won't you, Mr Sadoveanu?

MR SADOVEANU Indeed, yes, I am much relieved! It appears, Mr Hagglof, that during the 32 boards played by Messrs Rosswick and Brindley in this match no fewer than ten created some degree of suspicion. Would you say . . .

MR GARNER Objection! According to the report, five of those hands were struck out either before or after the committee had heard the player's explanation. We are concerned with five hands only, not ten.

MR SADOVEANU Then I will put the question in another way. Do you think it normal, or do you think it surprising, that after all explanations have been heard there should be five incidents in the course of 32 boards which leave doubt in the minds of an expert committee?

MR GARNER Objection! The witness has presented the report of a full committee, he should not be invited to add to the report any gloss of his own.

MR BASSETT I think that is right, Mr Sadoveanu. You may ask the witness to elucidate the report, not to add his own interpretations of it.

MR SADOVEANU I will ask a different question, not directly concerned with this report. When you watch a match on bridgerama, Mr Hagglof, does it happen often that you observe a bid, lead or play that causes you to wonder whether the players have some signalling system?

MR HAGGLOF No, very seldom.

MR SADOVEANU Very seldom, thank you. Now I want to ask you about the notation to one of the hands, which reads: 'Giving grounds for suspicion of a private understanding'. Why do you suggest that on this occasion there was a private understanding between the players rather than an exchange of signals?

MR HAGGLOF That was hand number ... ah, yes, I have it. Mr Brindley told us that his partner's bidding clearly indicated a particular distribution. There was nothing on the convention card to support this interpretation. Mr Brindley said it was impossible to describe all the inferences arising in their system.

MR SADOVEANU Then either explanation is possible: that there was an understanding not sufficiently explained, or that there could have been an exchange of signals?

MR HAGGLOF There could have been, but we decided to accept Mr Brindley's version.

Sadoveanu nodded and sat down – he had just drawn out the contents of the report without adding to it in any way. Garner, on the other hand, soon made considerable dents in it.

MR GARNER As editor of a magazine, Mr Hagglof, you have often conducted bidding competitions where a panel of experts give their answers to tricky problems. Do you sometimes find the experts at opposite ends of the pole, one saying that a certain bid is clearly correct, while another will describe it as ridiculous?

MR HAGGLOF That happens often, yes.

MR GARNER So you will agree that where correct bidding and play are concerned, everyone may have different opinions?

MR HAGGLOF That may be so in general, but here we were dealing with a small and specialized matter. We were not asking, what is the right bid, but what possible explanation could there be for the bid that was made?

MR GARNER Suppose that instead of your group of Scandinavian experts the committee had consisted of a group of, say, French and Italian, or Dutch and Belgian players: do you think they would have arrived at identical judgements about these disputed deals?

MR HAGGLOF No, but I think their general conclusions would have been similar.

MR GARNER You cannot be sure of that?

MR HAGGLOF No, not sure.

MR GARNER Now I come to my main criticism of your report. You appear to have studied the hands that, in your words, gave grounds for suspicion. Did you conduct an equally diligent search for hands that might dispel suspicion?

MR HAGGLOF Mr Brindley drew attention to one or two other deals to support his arguments, but no, we did not have time to examine the whole match for incidents pointing the other way.

MR GARNER Then I am bound to suggest that your report is of very little value indeed. For example, you mention a hand where a surprise lead of the unsupported king of spades turned out well. You imply that some signal may have been given. But suppose you had found another hand where the player led a spade with disastrous results, when there was a very reasonable alternative. That would be a very strong counter-indication, would it not?

MR HAGGLOF Yes, we were aware of this. That is one reason why we hestitated to draw any definite conclusions from the deals we studied.

MR GARNER I suggest that in this area negative indications are more significant than any positive indications can be. If the Chairman had not expressly forbidden any broadening of the discussion, I would have drawn your attention to some hands in other matches where my clients were by no means well inspired. I put it to you that your report is at best a half-report, with the more important half left out altogether.

MR HAGGLOF I have already conceded that the report is not as complete as we would have wished.

MR BASSETT Do you wish to re-examine, Mr Sadoveanu?

MR SADOVEANU One question only. Mr Garner has remarked that bridge players often have different opinions about the best bid on a particular hand. Nobody will dispute that. But here we are considering whether there can be any logical basis for the bid or play that was made at the table. In that area, would you expect so much difference of opinion between one expert and another?

MR HAGGLOF No. The members of the committee often disagree with one another on questions of bidding, but in this case we reached our conclusions with very little argument.

MR SADOVEANU In other words, Mr Garner was not comparing like with like?

MR HAGGLOF That is what I wanted to say, but I did not find the words so well as you, Constantin.

Sadoveanu twirled his moustache at this little compliment. He had weakened one of Garner's arguments but he had not answered the important one, the one dealing with the committee's failure to examine negative as well as positive indications. I had the feeling that Garner would argue that the whole report should be ignored because of this failure.

MR BASSETT Mr Garner, are you intending to ask Mr Rosswick or Mr Brindley to take the witness-stand?

MR GARNER I am going to call Mr Brindley, to explain the remark made in the coffee-shop which was overheard by the witness described as Mr Joe. That will only take a minute. Both players could speak extensively on the technical evidence, but this you have expressly forbidden. In my final address I shall contend that the case for the defence has been greatly handicapped by this ban.

MR BASSETT What about you, Mr Sadoveanu? Will you wish to cross-examine the players at length?

MR SADOVEANU Not at all, except possibly in relation to the evidence they give about the conversation in the coffee-shop.

MR BASSETT Then if you can limit your final speeches to about thirty minutes each, we will be keeping to schedule. Will you proceed, Mr Garner? What's that, Dave? Mrs Burton has been waiting for two hours? Oh, of course, your mystery witness. I'll ask her a few questions myself – let's hope she won't keep us for long. Ask her to come in, will you?

While Dave Hampton was walking to the door – it was quite a long walk because we were at the far end of a long room – I thought about the sub-committee's summary of the internal evidence. I had already looked at the five hands they quoted. The two play hands were, if anything, more suspicious than the example Elvin had given – but one had to remember that the main point he made was about the tempo of the play. It would have been useful to know whether the play on the hands from the Chinese match was fast, normal or slow. On the whole, I think the committee's summary was fair – the examples were certainly consistent with a signalling system but they didn't really prove it – and if the defence had been allowed to refer to other deals the overall effect might have been quite different.

It occurred to me that the sentence in the summary, 'In the committee's opinion the bidding and play of this pair is consistent with the exchange of unlawful information', was meaningless, because the most obvious bid in the world could be 'consistent with the exchange of unlawful information' – but if Garner had made that point he would have given Hagglof a chance to say that the bidding and play were of the kind one would expect if a pair had a cheating system.

Dave Hampton came back after a minute, and whom did we see emerging from the shadows, not an unknown Mrs Burton, but the motherly old soul who plays with Toni, Laura Durston. Dave must have misunderstood the name over the telephone. She was carrying her knitting with her.

MR BASSETT Why, it's Laura Durston, one of Hervey's back-room boys, or back-room girls, I should say. Our secretary made a slight mistake with your name, Mrs Durston. Will you take this chair? We must apologize for keeping you waiting so long.

MRS DURSTON Oh, I quite understand. Once when I had to give evidence in an unfortunate case in which my daughter was involved I had to wait around for two days. Today I had my knitting with me.

MR BASSETT Let me see, you probably know most of us in the room. After you have given your evidence you may be asked some questions by Mr Sadoveanu here and Mr Garner.

MRS DURSTON Everybody knows Mr Sadoveanu, of course, so tall and romantic-looking, and I know Mr Garner too. He was kind enough to give a ruling yesterday at a table where I was scoring, it was one of those rather puzzling situations where two bids were made simultaneously.

MR BASSETT May I ask, first, how you came to have any knowledge of the present affair?

MRS DURSTON It was in the Bulletin this morning, wasn't it? That the Appeals Committee would be meeting to consider a protest by the Chinese team?

MR BASSETT Yes, but how did you know what the protest was about?

MRS DURSTON I was scoring in the match between China and America on Sunday afternoon and again in the evening, so I could guess.

MR BASSETT I don't quite understand. Was anything said at the table?

MRS DURSTON No, but quite a lot was said afterwards.

MR BASSETT Do you mean that the Chinese players made some remarks to their opponents? This is the first we have heard of anything like that.

MRS DURSTON No, it was mostly between the Chinese captain and the small Chinese player with the horn-rimmed glasses.
MR GARNER That would be the gentleman with the consonantal name of Wch.
MR BASSETT They were talking in English, then?
MRS DURSTON No, in Chinese.

John Bassett was looking a bit baffled by now because Laura's answers seemed to be off the point – she wasn't helping him along at all. There was a slight pause, giving Harold Garner a chance to put his foot in it.

MR GARNER You'll be telling us next that you understand Chinese!
MRS DURSTON Yes, I do; just Cantonese, not Mandarin, I'm afraid. My husband, Ben, was in textiles; of course he's retired now. We used to spend two or three months every year in Hong Kong. I think it makes such a difference if one tries to learn the language, don't you? It was the same when we spent some time in India. A friend was saying to me only the other day that if the British in India had –
MR BASSETT I am sorry to interrupt you, Mrs Durston, but we must keep strictly to the matter in hand. We have reached the point at which the Chinese player and captain were exchanging comments at the end of the match. Did they know you could follow what they were saying?
MRS DURSTON Oh yes. Otherwise it would have been like eavesdropping, wouldn't it?
MR BASSETT I won't ask you what they were saying to one another because that would not be correct, but as a result of what you heard did you take any steps?
MRS DURSTON I thought about it a lot. You see, one or two little things had surprised me.
MR BASSETT But what made you think you could assist at this Inquiry?
MRS DURSTON I saw Mr Rosswick and Mr Brindley play again on the following day. I hope I am not being indiscreet, but there were some unfamiliar faces around. I could see they

weren't interested in the bridge itself, I did wonder if perhaps they were watching for something too.

MR BASSETT That was very observant of you, but please do come to the point: what is the evidence you wish to give?

MRS DURSTON To make everything clear, I think I must tell you what went through my mind at this stage. I wondered whether these observers, not being bridge players, would be looking for the right things. And I tried to work out three things If a signal was exchanged, when would it be done? What sort of information would it convey? And what form would it take?

Briefly, because you have told me you are in a hurry, I first thought that to be useful a signal must come early, before or during the first round of bidding. Often there is a choice of opening bid, I don't have to explain matters of that kind to you gentlemen. Secondly, I was sure the players would not be exchanging information about aces or about point count, that sort of thing comes out in the course of the bidding. Among good players distribution is the important thing, don't you agree? Thirdly, I thought the signal must be something very broad but at the same time natural — certainly not a gesture, because players cannot stare at one another, that wouldn't do at all.

I observed one or two things when I was scoring on the Monday evening, but something puzzled me and at the end of the session I obtained a copy of the match records and took it home with me. That was naughty, because really they are supposed to be kept in the press room. But in the early hours of the morning, by comparing the match records with some notes I had made, I found the answer I had been looking for. I found how the players were telling one another when they had a balanced hand — at least, fairly balanced, with no singleton or void.

MR BASSETT I think you should take over the examination now, Mr Sadoveanu.

MR SADOVEANU No, please carry on, Mr Chairman, we are all spellbound.

MR BASSETT In your view, what did a player do when he wanted to tell his partner he had no void or singleton?

MRS DURSTON Nothing.

MR BASSETT I don't quite understand. Nothing?

MRS DURSTON That's right. I must tell you what gave me the idea. It was that Mr Halley, some name like that, who wrote about hotels and motor-cars, there was one about aeroplanes, I saw it again on television quite recently. This book, the one that gave me the idea, was about banks. Did you know that the nightwatchman at a bank gives a *positive* message every so often to the police that everything is well, so if he is knocked on the head and *fails* to send a message they know something is wrong. Well, that was the answer here. The players were exchanging messages about distribution, as I thought they might be, and when they did *nothing* it meant no singleton or void. That was clever in a way, because you can't detect *nothing*, can you?

MR BASSETT I am becoming a little confused. If, as you say, they conveyed a message by doing nothing, there must have been occasions when they did *something*.

MRS DURSTON Oh, there were. As I said earlier, I was looking for some action, natural in itself, that would be easily observed by the partner. The idea occurred to me while I was knitting this cardigan I have with me now – no, I suppose you would call it a jersey; it's for my little grandson's birthday. My pattern calls for knit three, purl one, and it suddenly struck me, I've seen them make that kind of movement. Taking a card from one end to the other, I mean, like this. When they had sorted their cards, sometimes they would transfer just one card from one place to another. It didn't take long to work out the code.

MR BASSETT Indeed? What was the code?

MRS DURSTON I must tell you, I am not quite sure about voids, there were not enough examples while I was watching. Singletons I am sure about. A single card from one end to the other, left to right, showed a singleton in spades; the opposite way, right to left, a singleton in hearts; from middle to right, a singleton diamond; from middle to left, a singleton club. If you study it, there is a logical pattern in that code; the bigger movement for the major suits.

MR BASSETT Now that we have some positive evidence, you should take over the examination, Constantin.

MR SADOVEANU As you please, Mr Chairman. The next question must surely be, How did you establish a connection between, say, the transfer of a card from the left to the right and a singleton in spades?

MRS DURSTON Every time a gesture of this type was made, either by the player I was sitting behind, or by his partner, I made a note on my private scorepad, such as L to R. Later I compared three hands on which the L to R movement had been made, and the common feature was a singleton spade.

MR SADOVEANU I just want to be clear about the sequence of events. You have told us that you had your inspiration about what may be called the nothing-signal in the early hours of Tuesday morning. It follows that you must also have noted the positive aspects of the code. Did it not occur to you to inform someone in authority of your discovery?

MR GARNER Of her theory.

MR SADOVEANU Very well, of your theory?

MRS DURSTON I had to make absolutely sure, and I knew that the Chinese team was going to appeal, or had already done so. I thought the time to give my evidence would be when an Inquiry was held. Was that very wrong of me?

MR SADOVEANU I was not suggesting that at all. I just wanted to know your answer. Your witness, Mr Garner.

MR GARNER I want to ask you one or two questions, Mrs Durston, about your method of observation. When you were watching on Monday evening, say, during the match against Britain, you were sitting behind a player whose cards you could see, is that right?

MR DURSTON I was sitting behind Mr Brindley, yes, and I could see his cards. I remember I was quite surprised on one hand when –

MR GARNER So when his hand included a particular feature such as a singleton heart, and he made any kind of gesture, it was easy for you to think, Oh, that's what he does when he has a singleton heart?

MRS DURSTON That wouldn't be a very fair way to reach any kind of conclusion, would it?

MR GARNER No, it would not be fair, and I am not suggesting you did this deliberately, but it is a trap into which many so-called observers have fallen in the past. You see, you approached this matter with some preconceived ideas, did you not? Consciously or unconsciously, you had made up your mind what the signalling system was likely to be, according to your theories. Is that right?

MRS DURSTON Did it sound like that? I suppose it was, in a way. I thought the signal must be given early, so I looked for something that happened, something obvious but not suspicious, soon after the cards had been picked up.

MR GARNER You say, not suspicious. But is it not highly suspicious to sort the cards, then ostentatiously transfer one card from end to end? Is this not the sort of thing an observer would be bound to notice?

MRS DURSTON I don't think so. You must remember two things. First, a singleton in the hand of an individual player occurs on less than one hand in three. Second, many players, after sorting their cards, make at least one change, to prevent any possibility of an opponent drawing inferences from the way in which a card is played from the fan. The captain of our ladies team in Madrid last year warned us most particularly not to sort our cards exactly. I remember the example he gave. Suppose you draw the end card from the left of your hand, at any time in the play, and this card is a diamond, and later you play what is now the end card, a club. If you sort strictly by suits, an opponent may deduce that the diamond you played earlier was the only one you had left. I know I was quite shocked, because in fifty years of playing bridge I had never thought of such a thing. Also, the players in this case did not sort their cards, then pause and make an obvious movement. It was smoothly done, with no break in the rhythm.

MR GARNER Do you really expect us to believe that both players, while sorting their cards, which needs some degree of attention, were simultaneously working out the signal they had to give and looking for a signal their partner might or might not be giving?

MRS DURSTON The players followed a slightly different tempo in picking up their cards. The *second* player to speak sorted his cards and gave his signal quite briskly. The *first* player took more time, so that when he was ready to bid he had seen his partner's signal. They worked in relays, if you see what I mean.

MR GARNER It still seems to me a most awkward and unreliable way of conveying a message. However, none of this is important, for another reason. Do you not realize, Mrs Durston, that your evidence does not assist this Inquiry at all?

MRS DURSTON Why is that, Mr Garner?

MR GARNER Because evidence of this type is useless without corroboration. You say that certain gestures corresponded with certain holdings, but the moment is past, we will never know whether you deluded yourself or not. The proper course, if a code is suspected, is for one person to make a note of all the actions thought to be significant, and for another to compare those notes with the match records to see whether a pattern has been established. Do you understand what I am saying?

MRS DURSTON I think so. You mean that an outside person, someone not seeing the cards or knowing what the signals are thought to convey, should watch throughout a session and make written notes about all the gestures or movements?

MR GARNER That is an even better description of what I had in mind.

MRS DURSTON I'm so pleased. You see, my friend, Miss Trupp, did exactly that.

There was a gasp at this, even Miss Rootjens looked up from the machine where she was twiddling knobs to adjust the sound. Garner was stopped in his tracks and John Bassett put the next question.

MR BASSETT Are you saying that Miss Trupp — I know the lady you mean — sat opposite one of the players and made a note of each of the movements you have described?

MRS DURSTON Yes, during the second half of Tuesday afternoon. I was behind Mr Brindley, who was sitting North, and Miss Trupp sat fairly high up on the benches behind me, facing Mr Rosswick. All her notes related to Mr Rosswick's actions.

MR BASSETT At the time when Miss Trupp made her observations, what did she know of the supposed code?

MRS DURSTON Nothing, really. I simply wrote down the four actions I have described, the movement of a single card after sorting, and asked her to keep a record of what she saw. She wrote down the hand number, then either 'nothing' or a letter, ABC or D, describing one of the four movements.

MR BASSETT Did you subsequently go through the match records with her, to confirm your theory about the code?

MRS DURSTON I did that by myself as soon as the match records were available.

MR BASSETT With what result?

MRS DURSTON I'm sorry to say it was what I suspected. The signals agreed with the short suits in every case. I have all the notes with me here. It was the same with Mr Brindley, whose cards I could see. Each player held one void during the 16 boards. The signal appeared to be the same, but there may have been some additional signal to distinguish between singleton and void.

MR BASSETT Is Miss Trupp available to give evidence?

MRS DURSTON Let me see, it's ten to five. Virginia will be at the casino by now. Oh dear, she'll be quite cross with me if she is asked to leave when she is in a winning run, but she did promise to come if required.

MR BASSETT That may be necessary. Mr Garner?

MR GARNER You will appreciate that some of these developments have taken the defence by surprise. My friends and I would like a brief recess.

MR BASSETT I understand. If you go to that table at the far

end of the room you will be out of hearing. Meanwhile, the rest of us will relax and not discuss any aspect of the case during your absence.

Garner, Rosswick and Brindley were joined by Rudi Vector, the American captain, and the American delegate, who had been sitting wooden-faced at the committee table. I studied the hands again to see if they fitted with the theory that each player knew his partner's short suits. The one quoted by Elvin certainly did. Laura Durston resumed her knitting. After about five minutes Rudi came back without the others.

MR VECTOR Mr Chairman, there is no possibility at all of this Inquiry being terminated one way or the other before the semi-final is due to start this evening. In the circumstances my colleagues and I feel that the American team, in fairness to everyone, should withdraw from the competition. You will appreciate that this is in no sense whatsoever an admission that the case against the two players has been established. We feel simply that it would be wrong for the team to continue while there was the slightest doubt about the standing of any of the players.

MR BASSETT You mean you are giving Italy a walk-over? Very well, this Inquiry is adjourned. The committee will meet tomorrow morning at 10.30 to consider the next step.

   I understand that in addition to the journalists who lay in wait for us at the end of the morning session we now have to face a battery of photographers and radio reporters and television crews. I will make a brief statement, saying that as the matter has not been concluded the American team has most sportingly withdrawn from the contest. My own feeling is that the less any of us says at this stage, the better.

MR SADOVEANU May I say that I agree absolutely.

MR BASSETT I'm glad of that, Constantin. I'm told there's a special posse of photographers waiting for our dashing Rumanian.

John thanked all the non-committee people for their services, and asked me to take Laura to my room, away from the journalists and photographers. Laura was in tears when we reached the room – she said she hadn't wanted to give evidence at all but you couldn't let a couple of silly boys spoil the game for everyone, could you – Peter Rosswick was just weak, she was sure the other young man had led him into it. As soon as the coast was clear, I put her in a taxi and sent her home to Virginia's flat.

Most people thought the Americans had taken a dignified way out of an untenable position. However, Brindley rather spoilt the effect by saying in a television interview that the proceedings had been a farce from beginning to end, with evidence from a pack of gendarmes who weren't fit to control the traffic and a couple of barmy old Englishwomen who had read too much Agatha Christie.

Elvin was happy because his evidence had been confirmed and he had obtained a commission to write an article for one of the English Sunday papers – he was therefore grubbing around for every piece of gossip he could pick up. Maurice was looking very thoughtful – probably afraid people might wonder about his own partnership with Rosswick. I learned later that he had wanted to give evidence for the defence but old moneybags, Habib, had forbidden it – he wasn't going to allow two of his jockeys to appear on opposite sides.

Toni had spent most of the evening with Rosanna, so I didn't see her to speak to till the end of the session. I told her what had happened at the Inquiry and that everyone now assumed the players were guilty.

'How terrible!' she said. She was very upset. 'But I knew it would turn out this way. I looked up their birth-dates this afternoon. They're both Gemini.'

London and Deauville

by Elvin Starr

The telephone woke me up as usual. Bloody thing! Probably some other fool wanting to know 'what really happened in Monte Carlo'. Ever since my succulent piece in the paper last Sunday I've been getting calls from people I hardly know. I clambered out of bed and tottered to the machine.

'Mr Starr's residence,' I said in my Hollywood butler tone.

'Elvin, you awake?' Hell, it was Maurice. 'You hold queen to four, ace king to five, king x, two small. You open a heart, partner two clubs, you two hearts, partner two spades. Well?'

At least this wasn't difficult, even in my comatose state. I assumed the main point would come later. 'Three spades.'

'What would you say about four spades?'

'Agricultural.'

'What? Oh, yes. Well, that's what Miles bid with me at the club last night. I had ace to three, you can imagine. I'm telling you, he's gone.'

'It's true that he played poorly in Monte Carlo. He has things on his mind, I'm sure.'

'That's what Shoukry thinks. He says we mustn't play with Miles in the Prix Dupont at Deauville. I can tell you his exact words: "I am delighted to sponsor my system in the hands of dedicated experts, but I have no desire to support social butterflies".'

'But it's all fixed. Nothing we can do now.'

'You're forgetting paragraph 21, section 2, of our Agreement with Shoukry.'

'I am?'

'That's the one that gives him the right to nominate the team for anything except international events which are out of his control. He says, definitely, no Miles.'

'Even supposing we can shift Miles, which won't be easy, what's the alternative? Do we give Leonard the heave-ho, too?'

'No. Shoukry was impressed at Monte by Jim Orton. The one you call Haggis. He thinks Leonard and Orton would make a good pair.'

'Leonard wouldn't wear it. Apart from the fact that he and Miles are old friends, Miles is a good customer.'

'Shoukry's a better one.'

So that was it. To soften Leonard, Shoukry had put business his way.

'Who's going to break the news to Miles?' I asked.

'You are. Leonard and I both thought it would come best from you. I have to go now. *Shalom.*' I was left looking foolishly at the receiver.

I put on some coffee, washed a cup, and picked up the milk and daily paper. 'First Test Tube Quadruplets' and 'White Player Chosen For English Football Team' screamed at me from the front page. I turned to the more alluring contents on the inside pages, which set my thoughts running on familiar lines. I was feeling deprived because Toni was in the wilds of Yorkshire and Helga, till recently at any rate, in some Caribbean gin palace. Gavin was away, too, imbibing wisdom from an Indian sage. Helga was due back this week, so I decided to give her flat a try. After a couple of rings she answered herself.

'We arrived a couple of hours ago,' she said. 'Frank and I are dying to hear the dirt from Monte Carlo. It was in all the papers in our part of the world.'

'I've no doubt it was. When can I see you?'

'I'm going shopping this morning. You have lunch with me this time.' She named a restaurant in Mayfair. 'Meet me in the bar, about 1.15. Order me a Pernod if you get there first.'

Miles's London abode was in Culross Street, near Grosvenor Square, more or less on the way to my lunch date with Helga. If

I had to give him the bad news I might as well get it over. He was in when I rang and said, 'Come round by all means.'

I walked slowly along the mews, dagger in hand. Miles opened the door himself. 'I've had to let my man go,' he said with a sigh. 'I only have a cook and a cleaning woman now.'

'Times are hard,' I agreed.

Miles settled me into the best armchair and offered me a glass of Madeira, which struck me as a trifle old-fashioned. 'Have you heard the news about Ross?' he asked.

'Nothing recent.'

'You know he went from Monte Carlo to stay with some friends in Alsace? Last week he tried to kill himself by taking an overdose of heroin. Now he's in a hospital near Paris. He must be having a terrible time, because in France they don't ease you gradually out of drug addiction. It's cold turkey, no option.'

'Quite right, too.'

'Well, perhaps. But I feel desperately sorry for him. I'm not criticizing, but I couldn't have done what you and Laura did.'

You wouldn't have been clever enough to do what Laura did, I thought.

We had all assumed that Brindley, with his distrust of everyone else, had organized the cheating enterprise as a counterstroke, but Miles had been told by some friends in America that Ross had been the moving spirit. Apparently he had been desperate for money to maintain his drug habit and reckoned that as a world champion he would be able to charge the top price for pro dates. According to Miles, there would be no further inquiry. Brindley had resigned from everything and Ross was too ill.

It was time to approach the purpose of my visit. 'I was talking to Haggis last night,' I remarked casually. 'Porridge is playing in a Scottish team at Deauville, and Haggis wants to join our crowd.'

'One of us could play with him in the pairs.'

'I think he has his eye on the Prix Dupont. It might be a good idea, because last year you were complaining that you couldn't go racing in the afternoons.'

Miles isn't a fool. 'Last year there weren't any big events. This Prix Dupont is a different affair altogether.' He gave me a wary look. 'Have you called to tell me you want to change the team?'

'Of course not. The only question is whether we ought to have a fifth player. Shoukry says we can't rely on him because he has some business to attend to.'

'I suppose he put you up to this?'

'All he has said to me is that you seemed to have things on your mind.'

'He's right, I have. Don't muck me about, Elvin, I've been in this game too long for that.'

'Whether you've had a slight loss of form or not, the important thing is not to give the selectors a chance to break up our team before the trials for the next European. If we play as a team in Deauville and don't do well, they'll bring up the old cry of looking for fresh talent.'

'Leonard wouldn't play with anyone else. Have you thought of that?'

'He might, on the firm understanding that our team would be reunited for the European Championship.'

'Leonard has a sense of loyalty. However, I take your point. I'll speak to him myself. Consider it done.'

As soon as I was out of sight of Miles's house, I darted into a telephone box and called Leonard.

'Mr Fieldsman is tied up at the moment,' a prim voice informed me.

'Bondage in office hours? Shame on you both! Tell him it's Elvin Starr, phoning from Downing Street.'

Leonard came on the line a few moments later. 'What is it, Elvin? I'm busy.'

'Just this: when Miles calls you about Deauville, pretend you know nothing. Got it?'

'Roger. Goodbye.'

All this manoeuvring had been a strain on my nerves and I was glad of a drink when I got to the restaurant. Miles was an affected ass in some ways, but he had handled our conversation with dignity.

Helga entered the bar with a swinging stride that drew the eye of every man in the place. She was wearing a slinky tangerine number that showed off her tan.

'God, you look terrific,' I said. 'Tell me about your trip.'

'Later.' She summoned the waiter to fill up her glass. 'The rum drinks in the Caribbean are all right but they don't give you a jolt amidships like this stuff. Cheers! Now, tell me everything.'

When I came to Trupp's contribution Helga exclaimed:

'What blind fools they were! The mere sight of Virginia on the benches should have put them on their guard – Ross, anyway. She hasn't been known to kibitz a single hand in thirty years.'

This was true enough, it hadn't occurred to me. At the end of the story Helga asked:

'What do you make of the remark the man overheard – "We've got to change the system, they've begun to cotton on"?'

'Oh, I think the detectives were on to something there. Brindley and Rosswick probably noticed that I was discombobulated when I played against them and decided to make a change, but they didn't get round to it till later.'

'Did you know that Laura was going to give evidence?'

'No, I don't think anyone did. Hervey says she gave a logical explanation. The signal had to come early and it had to be some broad action, nothing that would require a close look. That's right if you think about it, but even so, Laura of all people!'

'I was in a train with her once, doing a fiendishly difficult crossword, and every time I read out an impossible clue Laura said "Well, dear, do you think it might be so-and-so?" and it always was. Some of us girls aren't quite so stupid as we look,' Helga added, batting her eyelashes.

'Then here's another test on female psychology: did you know that Julia and Rhoda were reunited? They're playing together in Deauville.'

'It doesn't surprise me. I never bought that story Toni told you, presenting Julia as a sort of female Wackford Squeers. Never mind Rhoda's coy protest, she and Julia were having a ball.'

You're dead right, I thought. The temptation to tell her of my own experience with Rhoda was gigantic but I managed to resist it.

We were on the *bombe surprise* now. Observing the faint white line between Helga's tits, I felt an urge to see the rest. When I made a delicate suggestion along these lines she hesitated for a moment, then said:

'Elvin, there's something I must tell you. First, about Frank. This holiday in the Caribbean wasn't just a pleasure trip. He's planning to buy a house there. For a reason. I don't suppose you know much about tax avoidance?'

'On the contrary, I'm an expert with an almost unblemished record.'

'I mean on a big scale. A new bill has been passed which will make a big difference to people like Frank. One of the scandal rags has been getting at him and he intends to stay out of the country till things quieten down. That's one thing I wanted to tell you. The other you may find difficult to understand.'

'Try me. I'm broadminded.'

'Well, you know how it is, those warm evenings in the Caribbean, waves lapping the shore outside our balcony, scent of syringa, or do I mean verbena? Anyway, it put new fire into Frank. He knocked me up, the randy sod.'

There was a misty look in her eyes and I guessed what was coming.

'I'm going to have the baby and go with Frank when he leaves the country. He's been different lately. So for you and me it's hallo and goodbye.'

'But we'll always be friends.'

'Don't be bitter, Elvin. It's time I gave up racketing around. I'll be back in London from time to time and we'll see one another then.'

I had to be content with that. Apart from a farewell party, I didn't see her again before she left.

In the end I didn't go to New York for the Cavendish Club Pairs. However, I collected £1,000 from Arthur Mainwaring as an advance for a share of my action. I also tried to persuade Mosey to cancel my £500 debt in exchange for a $12\frac{1}{2}$ per cent share, but this proposal fell on stony ground. In the weeks before Deauville I had to stay away from Knaves because the old fool Arthur wanted his money back and Mosey was making sour jests about the attractive proposition he had missed. I played some poker and backgammon, but that didn't go well either. One day in a chouette (a backgammon game involving three or more players) I took the cheque from the biggest loser and gave one of my own, of dubious quality, to the second biggest winner. The balloon would go up when I was in Deauville. All my hopes rested on the Prix Dupont, which carried the biggest prizes ever awarded in a bridge tournament.

Quite a large party from the club made the trip to Deauville. We took the bus from the rustic airport and bumbled along country lanes past the thatched barns, apple orchards, and the Charolais peacefully chewing their cud. We stopped briefly in Trouville and a few minutes later were in Deauville itself, admiring the elegant shops and half-timbered Norman houses. Some of our party dropped off at the Royal, where I had stayed the previous year. The rest of us went on to the Hotel du Golf. As the minibus chugged slowly up the final hill, Miles drew my attention to the pretty white bridge that crosses the road between the tenth fairway and the eleventh tee. I was determined to improve at this game.

The tournament began with a boring Individual, followed by a one-session team event, sponsored by a cosmetics firm. I was asked to play with the *Président d'Honneur*, a dignified old gentleman with white side-whiskers. We teamed up with Klaus Ellerman and Panos Spiliatakos – 'Orrible 'Airy.

The less serious team events in France are played in a relaxed way: you deal and play four boards against another team, comparing scores at the end of the round. We started well enough, then a hand occurred on which the *Président* left me in a transfer bid of four diamonds. I had a singleton ace of diamonds and when a trump was led and dummy went down with K x I couldn't help laughing.

'*Ne dis rien,*' said the *Président*. '*Vous facilitez le flanc.*' ('Don't say anything, you are helping the defence.')

The diamonds were divided 7-3 and I finished six down. At the end of the round Klaus and Panos came over to compare scores. When we came to the hand I had played in four diamonds Klaus announced the result at his table:

'600 for them.'

'600 for them,' I echoed.

'Impossible. For us.'

'No, for them. It was my fault. *J'ai facilité le flanc.*'

Despite this misadventure we finished third in a big field. The *Président* was delighted and 'Orrible 'Airy received a special cheer when he descended from the platform carrying a large bottle of perfume.

In the open pairs, which followed, I was drafted to play with Habib, who on this occasion was not accompanied by the Sultana. In this type of event you have to grab your opponents by the throat from the very first board. The Arab, bound by the dictates of his system, did not have the right technique and we were never in a challenging position.

Following a recent fashion on the Continent, the sponsors of the main event proposed to hold a fancy dress gala on the last night. During this first week we all paid stealthy visits to the representatives of a firm of theatrical costumiers. I planned to revive a schoolboy success as Captain Hook.

So far I was full of beans, playing golf every day and staying in the casino till four in the morning. Inevitably there was a reaction, and at the beginning of the second week I found I could sleep for only two or three hours a night. Habib gave me some tablets, warning me not to take any cheese or alcohol at the same time. They worked like a dream. On the eve of the Prix Dupont Maurice took me aside and gave me a little lecture. 'No more golf,' he said sternly, 'and no more late nights. There's £50,000 worth of prize money in this event.' I promised to be home by midnight, like Cinderella.

The next day began well with a call from Miles. 'Saved by the bell,' he said jubilantly. 'You know about that take-over bid for Monarch Furs? Well, Leonard rang his office this morning and they told him the deal had been forbidden by the take-over panel. The shares fell with a bump. We'll at least save our money on the options; better still, Mosey will lose his.'

The early rounds of the Prix Dupont consisted of a multiple team event, with four teams qualifying for the semi-final. We reached this stage without any special alarms and thought we had the better of the draw, but our match against the Swiss no. 2 team was close throughout. Two death-trap hands for our system occurred during the last quarter. The first cost us a lot of points and on the second we escaped only because an opponent let us off the hook. Maurice and I had warned Shoukry time and again that it was absurd to have to play guessing games at a high level in certain sequences, but he wouldn't agree to any change. When we narrowly escaped the second catastrophe I muttered something about the 'obstinate heathen'. I saw from Maurice's horrified expression that Habib was sitting behind me. If he heard, he gave no sign. We scraped home eventually by 7 match points. In the other semi-final the French no. 1 team beat Sweden.

The following day was a national holiday of some sort, so the final was not due to start till the evening. I had an inspiration: as Hervey, in his role of match manager, would have to superintend the dealing of the boards, what about asking Toni to come on a picnic? To my delight, she accepted at once.

Holiday or not, you are never deprived of an opportunity to spend your money in Deauville. I had no difficulty in hiring a car and finding a delicatessen shop, where I bought an appetizing selection of rough terrine, pastry boats crammed with langoustine, butter, a twist of new French bread, cheese, and a litre of young Beaujolais. Toni produced a rug and a thermos of coffee from the hotel. Imagine trying to lay on a similar spread in England on a Bank Holiday morning!

Toni looked ravishing in a sky-blue silk shirt with a halter neck and short blue shorts. Like many pretty girls who are not tall, she gave the impression of long legs and thighs. 'Your shorts are just the job for sauntering through the nettles,' I commented.

We set off in the direction of Caen. Pottering along at a steady twenty-five miles an hour, I considered my chances.

Picnics have a high success ratio in my experience; the world's dreary conventions seem remote and inhibitions are more easily broken down. But I mustn't press; Toni could not be forced but she might be nudged.

As the road curved away past Clairfontaine, the signs of civilization began to disappear. Cars gave way to an occasional tractor or an overburdened hay-wain, driven by a peasant with a face like a wrinkled nut. Before long I spotted the ideal place by the edge of a wood, with a stream close by. We carried the parcels and wine from the car and pitched camp under a leafy elm. The only sign of life was an inquisitive squirrel, which watched every move as we disposed of our goodies.

'Thank you, Elvin,' Toni murmured, as I poured out the last of the wine. 'That was perfect. Not even any midges.' She collected the remnants into a paper bag, then pulled the rug away from the shade of the tree, put on tinted glasses and stretched out in the sun.

'You look positively feline,' I said, slipping down beside her.

'You talk too much.'

I put an arm round her and kissed her lightly. Her response was not passionate at first, but warm and encouraging. Soon she began to breathe more quickly, her kisses became urgent, she responded to every touch. She was eager now, demanding and sinuously feminine, whispering words of love . . .

Late into the afternoon we lay there and for me the world didn't exist. Now I knew why I had chased this girl for a year.

As she was threading her way back into her shorts, she said suddenly:

'Tell me honestly, Elvin, were you disappointed? Would you say I was cold?'

'As the Sahara in a heatwave. What an extraordinary question!'

'Oh, good! You see, Hervey's been a pig lately.'

'In what way?'

'You remember those two hands for your system which you said were a death-trap? I was watching on bridgerama and it seemed very odd that two hands like that should turn up in sixteen boards. I said something about it to Hervey later. He was in charge of the duplication, of course. He flew at me as though I had suggested that he had slipped in those two deals to fix you and Maurice. We had a quarrel and he said some very hurtful things.'

'Is that when he said you were cold?'

'He said I was sexually frigid. Now I know it's not *my* fault that things haven't been right for us lately.'

It was a strange story because I had always thought of Hervey as being so cool and civilized.

Back at the hotel Toni went up to her room and I looked in at the bar, which was full of excited racegoers, most of whom seemed to have had a good day. Hamish MacBride gave me this account of his day at the races with Habib and Miles:

'In the taxi on the way there Sairr Miles is giein' a great spiel to the wee darkie, tellin' him that yin couldna beat ma carpet or that yin'll piss it. The wee darkie just sits there wi' a twinkle in his ee. After the firrst race an old geezer in a monkey suit comes up and says in English, Excuse me, gentlemen, may I have a worrd wi' you, Sooky? Milesy's ees are poppin' oota his heid, and when they go off he says to me, D'ye ken who that was, that was the Comte de Lasseeny, the biggest owner in France. Several other geezers come up to Sooky, suckin' his bum like it was icecream, and from then it was D'ye think this one is bred to stay, Sooky? and has this one any chance on the draw, Sooky? Whate'er the wee darkie says, Milesy backs it, and most of them win and Milesy comes awa' wi' thoosand-franc notes sprootin' oota his backside.'

While Porridge was talking I was giving Hervey some speculative looks out of the corner of my eye. Would he notice any change in Toni when he went upstairs? They say one can. Oh well, the squirrel wouldn't tell.

When I collected my key I found a cheerful postcard from Helga and a letter in an unfamiliar hand. A grubby piece of paper fell out; the writing looked as though a platoon of spiders were crawling across the page. When deciphered, it read:

Dear Mr Starr,

    I have lately suffered a very serious financial loss and therefore demand you to remit by return of post the sum of £490 you owe me from the pick-up game at Knaves Club on 16 December last when your team lost by 49 points and we had a bet of £10 a point. The post-dated cheques you gave me have been worthless as you well know. If I have not received same by the 18th inst. I will immediately report the whole matter to the Committee of the Club.

                     Yours truly,
                     B. Moisevitch

A product of the Letter-writer's Charm School, evidently. Thank God, my financial position wasn't so critical now. I'd be able to pay the little swine something even if we didn't win the final.

    The final was played over four fairly short sessions. The first two were level. On the second day Miles, who in the end had played for a different team and been knocked out, took the train to Paris and called on Ross, who was still in hospital. He told us at dinner that Ross was full of guilt, highly disorientated, and babbling about some confidential letter he was going to write to me.

    Maurice played below form in the evening and we began the last afternoon a few points down to our French opponents. The turning-point of the match came in the first half of the final session when I held

♠ K 10 8 7 4 3 2
♡ —
♢ 5 4 2
♣ A 6 5

I was South at game all and East, on my right, opened four notrumps. When I asked West what he understood by this, he said it was their variation of the old Acol four notrump opening. Different responses would indicate a specific ace or various combinations of two aces.

I passed, West bid five clubs, meaning no ace, and East bid six hearts notwithstanding. Obviously East thought he had only one loser, and as I had no *unexpected* trick (such as J x x x in a suit that an opponent might expect to be solid) I decided to sacrifice in six spades. Anything less than six down would show a profit as compared with a slam for their side, so it was not such a wild gamble. West doubled six spades and all passed. The bidding had been:

South	*West*	*North*	*East*
(Starr)	(Roche)	(Levine)	(Hausenball)
–	–	–	4 NT
pass	5♣	pass	6♡
6♠	dble	pass	pass
pass			

West led the 10 of clubs and Maurice put down as good a dummy as I could hope for:

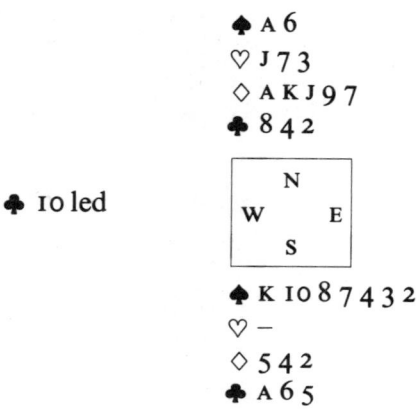

East overtook with the jack of clubs and I won with the ace.

What did I know about the hand? East had bid to six hearts without any promise of help from his partner. As our side held three aces, East must presumably hold two voids – a giant two-suiter consisting of hearts and clubs. Why had West led a club and not a heart, the suit his partner had called? The likely explanation, I thought, was that West had three hearts and a singleton club.

The picture was becoming clearer, but I checked the sequence of play again. The difference between first and second prize in this tournament was about £7,000, so I didn't intend to make a mistake. I thought sympathetically of the golfers one sees on television, playing a vital putt.

At trick two I led the 2 of spades, intending to put in the 6 if West played low, but he inserted the 9, forcing the ace, and East discarded a heart.

I ruffed a heart, finessed the 7 of diamonds (East was void, as expected), ruffed a heart, finessed the 9 of diamonds, ruffed the third heart, and finessed the jack of diamonds. Two clubs went away on the ace and king of diamonds and the last three cards were:

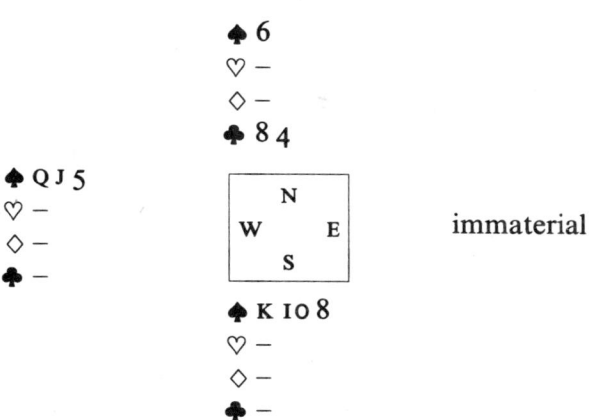

immaterial

I then ducked a spade and made the last two tricks. The full hand was:

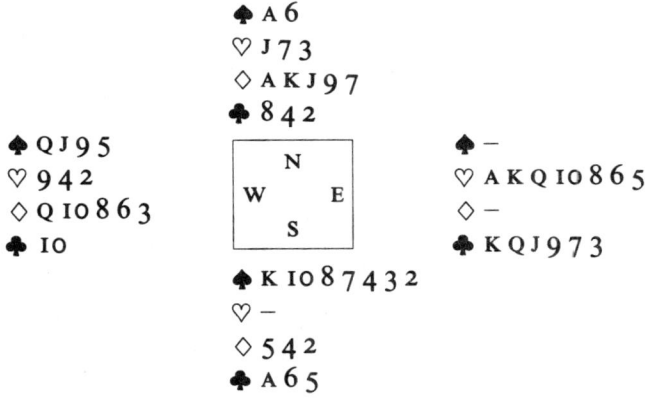

At the other table Leonard bid the East hand more cunningly and was allowed to play in six hearts doubled after South had been doubled in five spades. Making a doubled slam at both tables gave us a swing of 22 match points. With one set of 8 boards to go we were 15 ahead and feeling pretty optimistic.

'We haven't kissed the *mezuzah* yet,' Maurice warned me.

'And I have no intention of doing so,' I replied, with a glance at the stout Belgian lady who was scoring at our table.

'The *mezuzah*,' Maurice explained coldly, 'is a scroll that hangs in the home. A traveller kisses it on his safe return from a long and perilous journey.'

There were no further alarms and by six o'clock we were celebrating victory. 'When that six spade hand went up on the board I *said* you'd make it,' cried Toni, embracing me wildly. 'I *knew* you would,' said Miles, shaking me warmly by the hand.

There were celebrations in the bar of the casino and again at the hotel before we went to our rooms to prepare for the gala. We all had our costumes by now but had to share some items of make-up. I had a call asking for the loan of some spirit-gum, 'not for a moustache, but for eyebrow tufts'.

We had all been very secretive about our costumes. When the caller arrived and I saw a wide nautical hat filling the doorway I had to play the guessing game:

'Nelson? No, it's not an admiral. More like a captain.' Not a modern uniform. What captains could I think of, in fact or fiction? Hardy? Ahab? Hornblower? The turn-out was too smart for Hornblower. 'Bligh of the Bounty?' I noticed that the cheeks were puffed out with cottonwool. 'My God, it's Captain Bligh, in fact it's Charles Laughton as Captain Bligh. Marvellous!'

He smiled. No concealment was possible in my own case. My costume lay on a chair with a fearsome cutlass beside it. I had been practising with the hook, trying it on each arm in turn.

The Captain was carrying a bottle of wine and two glasses. 'A tot of rum would be more appropriate,' he remarked, 'but this is something special, a 1945 Hermitage.'

My visitor sat in a chair while I applied the spirit-gum. 'I was talking to the sponsors after the match,' he told me. 'They're interested in putting on a show in Rome, a match between the winners of the Dupont and the Italian team that won in Monte Carlo.'

'What are they offering?'

'Nothing's settled yet, but there'd certainly be a fee and a bonus for the winners. However, the main attraction is a possible television series. They could make at least a dozen half-hour programmes out of a long match.'

That was true. It would make a much better show than what they were doing at present – a scripted programme with actors as wooden as goalposts: 'I play the 3 of hearts'; 'And I play the queen of hearts'.

Bligh sipped his drink. 'This wine is delicious. Aren't you going to join me?'

'I ought not to. I'm still taking the sleeping-pills.'

'You haven't taken one this afternoon, have you?'

'No, of course not. I had one last night.'

'Then one glass couldn't possibly hurt you.'

'I suppose not.' I had drunk half a bottle at the picnic two days ago without any ill effects.

As I reached for my glass, the phone rang. It was the *Président*, with whom I had played in the earlier event. In case he didn't have a chance to speak to me at the gala he wanted to offer me his personal congratulations on winning the Prix Dupont. The session he had played with me had been a memorable experience, and so forth. It was kind of the old boy.

'There'll be plenty of drink circulating at the banquet,' I said when I rejoined the Captain. 'If you don't mind, I think I'll wait till then.'

'As you please. Tell me, have you had the mysterious letter from Rosswick yet?'

'No, not yet. What do you suppose it's all about?'

'Forgiving you?'

'You think so? For my evidence at the Inquiry? Could be.' Somehow I thought there'd be more to it than that. It occurred to me that Ross might intend to make some further damaging admission. He'd probably done something of the same kind before, with some other partner.

'Do you think now that you did the right thing in giving evidence?'

'I was steamed up at the time. Looking back, I do regret it in a way, but I think I was justified. I know some people have been saying "How could you do this to an old friend, a former team-mate?" There's another way of looking at it, isn't there? I mean, to use a cheating system against an old friend in a world championship is pretty bloody, too.'

'What do you suppose will become of Ross?'

'He'll be all right if he can get his health back. He need never be out of a job.'

'I hear that Brindley is bringing a series of lawsuits.'

'Nothing will come of it, you'll find.'

I had affixed the extra tufts of hair and the Captain's eyebrows were looking splendidly fierce. 'I must be pushing off,' he said. 'You'll want to get changed. Just a final toast before I go. Perhaps we'll meet again when you try to board my ship. It may be my painful duty to make you walk the plank. Cheers!'

I put out a hand – but it wasn't a hand, it was the hook, and I knocked the glass over.

'Sorry, I'll take the damned thing off,' I said, mopping up the mess and wondering how I would manage at the banquet.

'Don't worry,' said Bligh, pouring another glass. 'There's plenty left. You know,' he added reflectively, 'it was a damned good prize to win, wasn't it? I dare say the cash'll come in handy for you?'

'I should say so,' I laughed. 'And I'll tell you something: I've made up my mind never to get into that sort of hole again.'

'Very wise. Mind you, with a bit of capital behind you, you should be able to kill them at poker.'

The same thought had occurred to me. It's impossible to win at poker when you're worried about the money.

The Captain stood up. 'There's a match against the Italians and a million-dollar contract to look forward to,' he said. 'Let's drink to that. Cheers!'

'Third time lucky,' I said, clinking glasses. 'Cheers!'

When Bligh left I ran my bath and settled into it with a warm feeling of content. It was funny how everything had turned round in the last forty-eight hours: the reversal at Monarch Furs, the big win, the prospect of a television series and, most important of all, the apricot had blossomed at last with Toni.

Maurice had drawn my attention to something rather strange. It was a year to the day since the fiasco in Madrid when we threw away the European Championship in the last few boards. Toni would surely see some astrological significance in that.

I lay back and recalled the scene after today's match. All those people crowding round and congratulating me, how many of them were really pleased? Miles, Hervey, Habib, they all resented me for one reason or another. Who cares? I thought again of all the squabbles and petty jealousies among the top players.

Gosh, I feel tired. Unnaturally tired. Incredibly whoozy, in fact. Come on, I must get out of this bath, put on my pirate's garb, wrestle with that bloody hook. Hell, I can't get up. This is ridiculous. I don't want to end up like one of the Brides in the Bath.

That glass of wine was a mistake, after all. How can that be, when I haven't taken a pill since last night? Perhaps getting into a hot bath has made me dizzy. I mustn't panic, but I must get help. There's usually a bell somewhere in a hotel bathroom. Yes, there it is, half way up the wall. Pray God there'll be someone around at this hour to hear it.

I'm trying like mad to reach the bell ... my arm won't move an inch ... my whole body's numb. This is frightening. I need a doctor ... doctor ... doctor ...

It was a doctor who said, another sort of doctor, I know, who said, what was it, ah yes, I remember ...

I am sorry I have not learned to play at cards. It is very useful in life; it generates kindness and consolidates society.

Balls!

I can think of half a dozen couples in the tournament world who would willingly strangle one another. Sometimes the antipathy is natural, sometimes it can be traced back to a particular incident.

Like that board 27 in Madrid a year ago. If we had won the championship Hervey and I might not have broken up, Ross might not have gone to America, a lot of things might have been different ... It was like a pebble thrown into a pond, causing ever-widening circles ... circles ... circles ...

The Sentence

Mr Justice Lewthwaite continued his address:

'On 7 August 1992, a Monday, during a bridge festival at Deauville, Mr Elvin Starr mentioned that he had not been sleeping well. Mr Shoukry Habib gave him some tablets described as ...' The Judge consulted his notes ... 'ah, yes, I have it here, described as "mono amine oxidase inhibitors". Several witnesses have testified that Mr Habib warned Mr Starr that the tablets should not be taken in conjunction with cheese or alcohol. You were present yourself when this warning was given.

'On the last night of the festival Mr Starr, although a prizewinner, did not appear at the fancy dress gala. His hotel room was entered and his dead body found in the bath. It was clear at once to the medical examiner that he had suffered from some form of poisoning. The post-mortem the following day revealed both alcohol and a considerable quantity of the drug I have mentioned.

'The natural assumption was that during the celebrations that followed his victory in the bridge tournament Mr Starr either forgot the warning about alcohol or thought that a moderate amount, taken several hours after the pill, would not be dangerous. He might have taken the pill during the early hours of the morning to ensure a good sleep before the final stages of the tournament.

'There might never have been any suspicion of foul play but for one slight slip on your part. At about eight o'clock on the fatal evening, 13 August, the hotel porter received a call requesting that no message be put through to room *septante-six*, this being the number of Mr Starr's room. The same request was made to the switchboard. The porter said in his evidence that to him one English accent sounded much like another, but he recalled the incident because the caller, whom he assumed to be the occupier of the room, said *septante-six* instead of *soixante-seize*. The word *septante*, for seventy, is used in Belgium but never in France. Mr Starr, who was reasonably fluent in the language, would certainly not have made this mistake. The French authorities – it was most astute of them, I consider – realized that the call had been made by a different person and that this might be significant. They at once intercepted all bottles and glasses before they passed through the kitchens. They discovered a wine bottle and a glass that had traces of the drug. Monsieur Bourdin, manager of the *Vieux Vignes*, has identified you as the purchaser of the bottle in question. He gave us an account – indeed a lengthy account – of the conversation that took place when you ordered three bottles of 1945 Hermitage, a particularly heavy wine.'

'Counsel for the Crown has reconstructed the scene as follows:

'You poured yourself a normal glass of wine, then mixed the drug in the same or another bottle and took it, with a second glass, to Mr Starr's room. You carried the bottle and glasses away with you when you left and a few minutes later you put through the two calls to the porter and the switchboard to prevent any possibility of interruption while the drug was taking effect.

'It is clear that the poisoning was deliberately and cunningly planned. Until recently a killing that resulted from a felonious act was, without qualification, murder. The Law now makes certain distinctions between first-degree murder and second-degree murder. Where death results from a felonious act but may not have been intended, it is possible to bring in a verdict of second-degree murder.

'Your Counsel has argued, in his alternative plea, that you did not understand the risk and intended to do no more than cause distress. As to that, inquiries have revealed that you yourself have had this drug on prescription and must have been aware of its properties.

'Although the Law is concerned with intent, not motive, it is impossible to consider one without the other. Counsel for the Defence has laid much emphasis on the apparent absence of motive for so extreme a crime. Counsel for the Crown has put forward as a motive the conventional explanation that you were jealous over a woman. In the course of your own testimony you rejected that explanation. To normal people it would scarcely seem possible that resentment over the break-up of a bridge partnership, and envy of your former partner's successes, could lead in the end to murder. Nevertheless, after listening to the various witnesses I have come to the conclusion that this was, indeed, the dominant motive.

'Be that as it may, I cannot accept that you were unaware of the likely consequences of your action. It is therefore my duty to sentence you, Hervey Pearson, to death for the first-degree murder of Elvin Starr. A physician appointed by the State will administer a fatal drug. May God have mercy on your soul.'